For Elaine
Bless

MW00710359

A SICILIAN FAREWELL

A NOVEL

BY

MaryAnn Diorio

VOLUME 2 OF *The Italian Chronicles* TRILOGY

TopNotch Press
A Division of MaryAnn Diorio Books
Merchantville, NJ 08109

A SICILIAN FAREWELL
by MaryAnn Diorio

Volume 2 of *The Italian Chronicles* **Trilogy**

Published by TopNotch Press
A Division of MaryAnn Diorio Books
PO Box 1185 Merchantville, NJ 08109

Publisher's Note: This is a work of fiction. Names, characters, places, and incidents either are the product of the author's imagination or are used fictitiously. Any resemblance to actual persons living or dead, business establishments, events, or locales is entirely coincidental.

Some Scripture quotations are from the ESV® Bible (The Holy Bible, English Standard Version®), Copyright © 2001 by Crossway, a publishing ministry of Good News Publishers. Used by permission. All rights reserved.

Some Scripture quotations are taken from the Holy Bible, New Living Translation, Copyright ©1996, 2004, 2007, 2013, 2015 by Tyndale House Foundation. Used by permission of Tyndale House Publishers, Inc., Carol Stream, Illinois 60188. All rights reserved.

Softcover Edition: ISBN: 978-0-930037-23-9
Electronic Edition: ISBN: 978-0-930037-37-6
Library of Congress Control Number: 2016916123

While the author has made every effort to provide accurate telephone numbers and Internet addresses at the time of publication, neither the publisher nor the author assumes any responsibility for errors or for changes that occur after publication. Further, the publisher and author do not have any control over and do not assume any responsibility for author or third-party websites or their content.

Cover Design by Lisa Vento Hainline.

Praise for the Fiction of MaryAnn Diorio

The Madonna of Pisano

"From the first couple of pages my emotions were pushed into chaos. I keep wondering at how easy it is for people to believe a lie and allow doctrine to be their truth…. This is one beautiful story that makes Christ the Redeemer shine so brightly."

~ *Amazon Customer*

"Excellent characters, dramatic plot. Beautifully written, giving wonderful feeling for the setting in place and time. Emotionally intense situations, satisfying resolution. Among the two or three best novels I have read this year. Highly recommended."

~ *Dr. Donn Taylor, Novelist and Former Professor of Literature*

Surrender to Love

"I enjoyed reading *Surrender to Love* by MaryAnn Diorio. It was a short story that packed a powerful punch. Anyone who has ever experienced loss in their life, in any form, can automatically relate to the feelings of Teresa and Marcos in this book. In addition, there were three characters, each of whom experienced significant loss—but each from a different perspective; this brings even more depth to the book. It showcases how, despite knowing "what to do," it's not always easy to tell your heart to do what your head knows it should. And that saying goodbye can feel like a betrayal of sorts…letting go of the old is more than just head knowledge—it has to come from the heart, a full surrender."

~ *Cheri Swalwell*, Book Fun *Magazine*

"I was immediately drawn into the story of this young woman whose future and plans were cut short. The grief that she felt and refused to address applies not only to lost loved ones, but also to unexpected situations or challenges in life. The discovery of hope is most satisfying, leaving you wanting to share in her newfound joy."

~ *Deb, Amazon.com*

A Christmas Homecoming

Winner of the Silver Medal for E-Book Fiction in the 2015 Illumination Book Awards Contest sponsored by the Jenkins Group

"This short story is a wonderful way to start the Christmas season. It is a story full of human emotion and the struggles this life can challenge us with. The lesson throughout the story is that all things are possible through God's grace. This is a 'feel good' story that lifts the spirits and keeps you encouraging the main character to persevere and not give up. It is a great book for a short respite from our busy lives."

~ Kimberly T. Ferland, Amazon.com

"Well-woven. If only all stories made me sit on the edge of my seat, unsure of the outcome, but desperate for a good conclusion for the characters!"

~ Sarah E. Johnson, Poet

"A great Christian read. A powerful short story packed full of love, hope, heartbreak and a strong message on forgiveness."

~ Jerron, Amazon.com

ACKNOWLEDGMENTS

Books are the fruit of the efforts of far more people than simply the author. Books are born from the combined efforts of many people with multiple talents, all of whom pool their resources to produce a work that is worthy of its readers. Such, I trust, is the case with this novel you are holding in your hands.

Above all, I would like to thank God my Father in Heaven for giving me the idea for this book. He is the Giver of every good gift. This story is a gift from His heart to mine. Thank You, Father, for entrusting me with Your gift. I worship You!

I would like to thank my Lord and Savior, Jesus Christ, for sustaining me as I wrote this book. Lord Jesus, You are the Awesome Redeemer, the One Who makes all things new. Thank You for renewing me as I wrote this story. I praise You!

I would like to thank Holy Spirit, my precious Guide and Counselor, as He unfolded to me this story of His heart. I could feel His Presence hovering over me as I wrote. Thank You for guiding me on this creative journey and pointing me in the direction of Your choosing. I adore You!

Heartfelt thanks are also due to my superstar husband, who did much of the historical research that serves as the background for this novel and who did the grocery shopping, the cooking, and the cleaning as I worked tirelessly "in the zone."

A very special thanks to my editor, Mr. Frank Kresen, whose insightful comments made this story so much stronger because of his editorial skills.

Deeply, deeply loving thanks to my precious daughters, Lia Diorio Gerken and Gina Diorio, who prayed me through the tough times. I am so honored to be your Mom. You are the best!

Last, but certainly not least, sincere thanks to my precious readers. Without you, this book would have no home. May its home be your heart. May it bless you and touch the deepest places within you with the redemptive and healing love of Jesus!

DEDICATION

To Dom…

My Man of Steel and Velvet

A SICILIAN FAREWELL

"If you cling to your life, you will lose it;
but if you give up your life for me, you will find it."

~ Matthew 10: 39 NLT

A Sicilian Farewell

by MaryAnn Diorio

Pisano, Sicily, 1896

Chapter One

Dusk fell in Luca Tonetta's tailor shop as he counted his meager earnings from his past week of work. His revenue had dropped fifty percent in the last week alone. Not good. Especially since he had a wife and three young children to support.

And two months of back rent due to his landlord, Silvestro Lamponi, the man who owned the building in which Luca's shop was located.

At this rate, Luca would soon be bankrupt if he didn't do something fast.

Besides, Silvestro was none too happy and had made it clear that, if Luca did not pay up, he'd be evicted.

Luca's stomach tightened as he returned the few coins to the leather pouch in which he kept his earnings. Prospects for a financial turn-around here in Pisano were few and far between. With Italy's recent devastating defeat at the hands of Ethiopia in the Battle of Adwa, Sicily had felt the blow more than the mainland. No wonder so many were leaving the island for better opportunities elsewhere. The newspaper headlines that very morning had warned of an imminent economic collapse and reported a mass exodus of men from the island.

Luca rubbed his face. What would the mass exodus

mean for his business? Already, the clothes racks of his tailor shop, usually full of finished projects by the end of the day, now held only a few items, while the coffers at the end of the workday held one-fourth the revenues compared to this same date a year ago. In recent weeks, the number of customers had dwindled drastically as more and more men left Pisano—and the entire island—for better opportunities abroad. At first, it had been the lure of wealth that drew them. But now, it was the lure of survival.

Luca raked his fingers through his hair. He had to do something fast—something that would allow no option for failure. If he failed in his role as provider and protector, he'd never be able to look at himself in the mirror again. Nothing else mattered more.

As if the economic decline were not bad enough, productivity from *Bella Terra*, his wife's family farm, had dropped drastically. Last spring's drought had nearly destroyed the entire orange and lemon crops, and their vegetable staples of green peppers, zucchini, and string beans had fallen far short of yielding their usual bounty.

Things did not look good.

Luca exhaled a long breath. What could he do that would assure him of financial success and, at the same time, not put his family in difficulty? Should he join those who were leaving the island, or should he make a last-ditch effort to rescue his business from a looming death?

The latter choice seemed pretty bleak. Among the large numbers of the population leaving Sicily—and especially Pisano—were those who would have been potential customers.

He shook his head as the weight of the decision settled in the pit of his stomach.

He placed the leather pouch in the wooden box where he stored his weekly earnings and locked it. The thought of having to close the tailor shop he'd taken over from his late father and built to a thriving business sickened him. Made him feel like a traitor to his father.

And a coward in the face of challenge.

Luca's mouth went dry. Yet, what was worse: Leaving Sicily for work in America or facing the collapse of his business?

He drew in a deep breath. Perhaps the better part of valor would be to join the emigrants. Reports had already trickled back from fellow Sicilians in America that wages there were three times what they were in Sicily. Tripling his wages would mean enough not only to feed his children but to educate them as well.

And to allow his wife Maria to buy a new pair of shoes once in a while. Not that she ever complained, sweetheart that she was.

He rubbed a hand across his forehead and turned to his young son Nico, working at his side. "Meager earnings this week."

Nico looked up from the trousers he was pressing, his thick, dark brows furrowed into a question. "Sorry, Papa. What can I do to help bring in more customers?"

Luca smiled at this wonderful son of his heart, if not of his flesh. "It's not that customers are lacking. People still need their clothing altered or repaired, even if they want to forego a new suit of clothes. The problem is that money is lacking. People don't have the money to spend on having suits made or clothes altered. Sicily's economy is fast collapsing."

Nico placed the iron on its trivet. "What are we going to do, Papa?"

Luca knit his brows together. "Looks as though more and more of our men are leaving Sicily."

"Why?"

"The economy of our island is in fast decline. Between Italy's recent defeat in Ethiopia and our government's mismanagement of funds, it's becoming more and more difficult to support one's family. As a result, our men are leaving for America, England, and other parts north."

"Will we have to leave, too?"

Luca placed his arm around his son's shoulders. At eleven years of age, the boy was fast growing into a man. "I don't know, son. To be honest, I have been thinking about it." He gave Nico's shoulder a squeeze. "Thinking about it quite a bit. I'm concerned that, before long, I won't be able to make enough of a living here to take care of our family."

Nico's eyes widened. "It could be exciting!" His lips broke into a smile.

Luca smiled back. "Yes. Indeed, it could." Nico had a childlike faith that inspired Luca. "I guess it depends on how one looks at the situation. There's a lot at stake. A lot I have to think about as the head of the family."

"What do you mean?"

"I mean that if Sicily's economy collapses, I will be left without a means of earning a decent living. And that would mean it would be difficult to take care of you, Mama, and your little sisters."

"But God will provide for us. You always tell us to remember that."

"Indeed, He will, son. But sometimes He provides by sending us to where the provision lies."

Luca patted Nico's head. "My honor as a man, a husband, and a father demands that I do all I can to take care of you." Luca's voice caught. "I would no longer respect myself if I did not do everything possible to take care of my precious family."

"I respect you, Papa."

Luca's heart warmed. One thing he never wanted to lose

was his son's respect.

Nico grew pensive. "What would happen if we don't go to America?"

"We would likely go bankrupt."

"Then we should go to America. That settles it."

Luca smiled. "Thank you, Nico. But I will seek God's will in the matter. One does not uproot one's family simply out of a desire for more. Unless God is in this, I won't make a move."

A broad grin crossed Nico's face. "Moses once said the same thing. I read it in the Bible."

Indeed. So, Luca would be in good company by waiting on the Lord for a confirmation of His will.

Nico returned to his pressing. "In geography class, I've been learning about other countries of the world. The world is so big, and there are so many beautiful places to see. Imagine how wonderful it would be to see them in person instead of only in a book."

Luca pondered his son's words. Convincing Nico to leave Sicily would be easy. But convincing Maria? That would take a miracle.

"Yes, my son. God has created many beautiful places on this earth. To be able to see them is a blessing." Luca cleared the counter in preparation for closing the shop for the day. "But I'm not sure how your Mama would feel about leaving Pisano and, especially, *Bella Terra*. She's spent her whole life here."

Nico laughed. "That's precisely the reason she should leave." He placed a hand on his father's arm. "Besides, Mama loves you. She'll go wherever you go."

Luca hoped that were true. But when he saw how happy Maria was after five years of marriage and two more children besides Nico, he had his doubts. Even though she'd loved him enough to marry him, she'd had reservations when, before their marriage, he'd told her he was planning to go to America. His simple mention of it had been enough for her to refuse his marriage proposal. Only when he'd decided to remain in Sicily had she agreed to marry him.

But now, what would she do if he told her he thought God was calling him to move his family to America?

A shudder ran through him. He locked the cash drawer and placed the key on the hook hidden underneath the counter. "Your Mama loves Sicily almost as much as she loves me."

Nico looked up from his work. "*Almost* means she loves you more."

Luca chuckled. Over the years, the boy's incessant optimism had brought great joy to his life. "Well, I'll talk with Mama about it and see what she says. But my hunch is, she'll think it's a bad idea."

"You don't give her enough credit, Papa. Mama is practical and level-headed. Once you convince her that moving is the best thing for the family, she'll go along with the idea."

"I hope you're right, son." Luca sighed. "I certainly hope you're right."

"I'll pray, Papa. God will show you the right thing to do."

Truth was that God *had* been showing Luca what to do for a good while now. But Luca was struggling to obey Him. *Lord, give me a sign. I need a clear and unmistakable sign.*

"Thank you, my son. Praying is always a good thing to do. Especially before making a big decision."

But would God answer Luca's prayer in time to avoid a catastrophe?

* * * *

Shortly before closing time, the loud clang of the shop

doorbell interrupted Luca's thoughts.

"*Buona sera, Signor* Luca." Sergio, the postman, entered with a letter in his hand.

"Good evening, Sergio. You're working late, today."

The postman smiled. "My job demands good service for my customers." He handed Luca a letter. "This is for you. From America."

Luca's heart stirred. "From America? I wonder who it could be." Luca took the letter and read the return address. *Giulio Genova.* A chill ran through him. Could this be the sign for which he'd prayed? Luca looked up at Sergio. "A former customer of mine from Trapani. He now lives in America."

"America, eh? I've been thinking of going there myself."

"Have you? I've been thinking the same thing."

"With the way things are going in Sicily, it's a wonder there's anyone left here. Two of my brothers have already left for England, and another will be moving to Milano. The economic situation looks pretty bleak."

Luca nodded. "Indeed, it does. Business has fallen drastically over the past year. I've been praying about what to do."

"You're a good man, Luca." Sergio patted Luca on the back. "Would you throw in a little prayer for me, too?"

Luca chuckled. "Of course, my friend. But you can talk to God yourself, you know."

"Yes, I know. But somehow I think he hears those who are holier. Like you."

"Scripture says that all of us have sinned and fall short of the glory of God."

Sergio smiled. "Well, I've fallen far shorter than you, my friend. See you later."

"Thank you, Sergio."

"My pleasure. Enjoy your evening." Sergio nodded

toward Nico. "A fine young son you have there. Takes after his father."

Luca only nodded. When Nico turned twelve, Luca and Maria would tell him about his birth father. "Thank you, Sergio. Nico is, indeed, a wonderful young man."

Sergio tipped his hat and left, clanging the shop doorbell behind him.

Nico rose and stood beside Luca. "Wow, Papa! A letter all the way from America!"

Luca's hands trembled as he broke the seal and opened the letter. Could this, indeed, be the sign he'd asked of the Lord?

Luca unfolded the onionskin paper and began to read:

Dear Signor Tonetta,

Greetings from America! I hope you remember me. I am Giulio Genova, an old customer of yours. You altered a suit for me shortly before my departure for America almost six years ago. I trust you are doing well. I also hope you have found a good wife since I last saw you.

Luca smiled as he remembered Giulio's parting words about finding a wife. Wait till he met Maria. If, that is, Maria would be willing to leave her beloved homeland. Luca's pulse raced as he continued to read.

I am now living in Brooklyn. The city is teeming with opportunities, especially for skilled tailors. In fact, my boss, Will Dempsey, a clothing contractor in Brooklyn, is looking to hire another tailor. I told him about you, and he is willing to give you a job. If you are interested, you would need to begin work on the first of October.

I also know of an empty flat for rent in my own tenement house. The flat is in the same building as Mr. Dempsey's workshop. The landlord is willing to hold the flat for you if you let me know by the first of

August whether or not you would like to rent it. Of course, he would need an advance deposit.

I wanted to let you know all of this in case you are still considering moving to the new Promised Land. Now is the perfect time to do so, my friend. If you do decide to come—and I hope you will—please write to me at the address on the letter. Above all, I want to keep my promise of cooking for you the best Italian meal on this side of the Atlantic.

Sincere regards,

Giulio Genova

Luca smiled, clearly remembering Giulio's enthusiastic promise to cook him an Italian meal should Luca ever visit him in America.

Luca slowly folded the letter. His heart was full. Surely Giulio's letter was a sign from God confirming what Luca had been sensing in his heart. The Lord was telling him to go to America. He was making His will clear.

He was preparing every step of the way.

"What did he say, Papa?"

Luca turned to Nico. "He said his boss is looking for skilled tailors and is willing to hire me. Giulio also said he knows of a place where we could live, right in the same building where I would work. I simply need to let him know what I decide."

"That's wonderful, Papa! See. God is working out all the details. It must mean we are to go there."

Luca placed a hand on Nico's shoulder. "I have yet to talk with your mother about this. I'm not so sure she will be as excited as you are." He tousled Nico's hair. "Now go finish the pressing so we can go home."

Still holding Giulio's letter in his hand, Luca approached the front window facing the square to close the wooden shutters. A palpable haze of tropical heat hovered over the square, reluctant to make way for the evening breeze.

Luca gazed over the familiar square before him. The square where he'd spent a good portion of his life plying the tailor trade. Most of the shops had already closed for the day, leaving the square empty and darkened, except for the single gas lamp that illumined the white marble fountain. A lone pigeon, bobbing its smooth, gray head, ambled around the circular base of the fountain in search of a fallen crumb of bread. The village vendors of vegetables, fruit, and fish had already closed down their wooden stalls and left for their hillside farms to rest, gather, and replenish their supplies for the following day. The next morning, they would return at the break of dawn to repeat what they had done today.

Life went on as usual, day after normal day. But things were changing in Pisano. Luca sensed it. And, like it or not, he would have to adapt to the changes in order to survive.

Unless, of course, he left.

He studied the wide expanse before him. Behind the distant mountains, the setting sun wove a delicate thread of yellow, orange, and crimson just above the purple-blue peaks.

Luca gazed at the familiar scene. What lay beyond those mountains? Why did he feel an increasing urgency to find out? To what destiny was God calling him? And his family?

And why?

He drew in a deep breath, closed the shutters, and then turned to his son. "Time to close up for the day. Mama will be wondering where we are. You know how she hates for us to be late for dinner."

Nico nodded. "I'm finished, Papa. I just have to hang up these trousers and then we can leave."

Luca watched proudly as Nico carefully folded the well-pressed trousers, placed them neatly over a hanger, and hung them on the finished-projects rack.

Luca's heart warmed. The boy was learning the tailoring trade well. Plans were for Nico one day to take over the family business, just as Luca had taken it over from his father. But would there be a business to take over? Or would this precious son of his find a better opportunity for success in a new world?

Only time would tell.

Luca shook his head. No. Not only time.

But Maria's reaction as well.

* * * *

"Valeria, please play with your baby sister while Mama finishes cooking. Papa and Nico will be home soon and will want a good meal."

Maria Landro Tonetta stirred the spaghetti sauce with one hand while, with the other, she motioned to four-year-old Valeria to keep two-year-old Anna occupied.

Maria smiled as she glanced at her two beautiful little girls, both the fruit of her deep love for Luca. Marrying him and bearing his children had been the greatest joys of her life. She could not be more content. She had it all. A wonderful husband. Beautiful children. A home she loved in a country she deeply loved. What more could she want?

"Maria, we're home."

The sound of Luca's voice still made her heart flutter, even after five years of marriage.

He strode into the kitchen, took her in his arms, and kissed her soundly on the lips. "How is the love of my life?"

"Happy you're home. Dinner will be on the table in a minute." She removed the cast iron pot of spaghetti from the wood stove and poured off the boiling water into an empty basin to cool. After dinner, she'd empty the basin of water on the ground outside to nourish the roses in her rose garden. Pasta water was full of nutrients.

She placed the cooked spaghetti in a large, brown ceramic bowl, poured the marinara sauce over the spaghetti, sprinkled a handful of grated Parmesan cheese over it, then mixed the pasta well with two forks before bringing it to the table.

Luca and Nico washed their hands then sat down to eat.

Luca patted his stomach and smiled. "This looks delicious! And the aroma drew me all the way from the village."

Maria laughed and gave him a teasing slap on the shoulder. "Don't be silly. There is no way you could have smelled the aroma from the village."

"Oh, but I did!" Luca gave her a mischievous grin.

"And I did, too, Mama." Nico joined in the family fun.

Maria burst into laughter. "Then you two have the sharpest noses in all of Sicily."

"I have a sharp nose, too, Mama." Valeria tapped her nose and giggled.

Maria's heart filled with joy. How blessed she was! There was nothing more she desired.

She smiled at Luca. "I made the pasta just the way you like it. *Al dente.*"

"And God made you just the way I like it."

She warmed from head to toe. What a romantic husband she'd married! He always said the right thing at the right time.

Maria placed Anna in her high chair while Valeria climbed up on a chair next to Luca and adjusted herself on the raised cushion.

He reached over and gently pinched her little cheek. "How's my little angel today?"

Valeria wiggled in her seat. "I helped Mama take care of Anna."

Luca smiled broadly. "What a good little girl you are to help your mama like that. I'm sure she was pleased."

Anna clapped her plump little hands in agreement.

Luca grinned at his youngest child. "I see you were pleased, too, Anna."

Luca reached for Maria's hand. "Let's pray. Heavenly Father, we thank You for the food we are about to eat. Sanctify it by Your grace. May it nourish us so that we can continue to do Your will as long as we are on this earth. In Jesus' Name we pray. Amen."

"Amen." Maria's heart warmed every time Luca prayed. How thankful she was for a Godly husband who wanted nothing more than to obey God and to serve Him faithfully! She was, indeed, a blessed woman.

She took Luca's plate and filled it with a generous portion of spaghetti. Next she served Nico and then Valeria and Anna. Finally, she took a portion for herself.

Anna began to pick up the spaghetti with her hands. "Anna, no!" Maria quickly reached over to her youngest. "Mama will cut the pasta for you."

Luca rose from his place. "Here, let me do it, Maria. Relax and enjoy your meal. I'm sure you're tired from running after two little ones all day." He finished cutting Anna's spaghetti then sat down again.

He turned to Maria. "How was your day?"

"The usual. Taking care of the children. Cooking. Doing laundry." Maria swallowed a forkful of spaghetti then turned to Luca. "Oh, by the way, Don Franco said he will be leaving us."

Luca looked up from his plate, his eyes round with surprise. "Really? Why is that?"

"He's been offered a job as headmaster of a private school in Milano. The pay is much better than what we can afford to give him. He doesn't want to leave, but with the economy declining the way it is, he feels he has no choice." Maria rolled another forkful of spaghetti. "I'm sorry we can't pay him more to manage *Bella Terra*. He's been a faithful foreman."

"Indeed, he has. He did a great job of restoring the farm to its former station. Almost an impossible task."

Maria nodded. "I don't know how we're going to replace him."

Luca put down his fork. "We may not have to."

Maria stopped short, her blood turning to ice. "What do you mean? We need a foreman to oversee the workers."

Luca leaned forward. "I received a letter today from Giulio Genova, a former customer of mine who emigrated to Philadelphia in America. He has since moved to Brooklyn, New York, and wrote to tell me that his boss is looking for experienced tailors."

Every muscle in Maria's body tensed. "So? What does that have to do with us? You have a business right here in Pisano, and we have the farm. There's absolutely no reason for us to leave." Her voice was firm and decisive.

"Maria, things are changing rapidly in Sicily. This morning's headlines predicted an economic collapse. My earnings this past month were one-quarter of what they were a year ago at this time. If the situation does not improve, we will go bankrupt. Business is dropping off as more and more people leave the island for other parts of the world. It's becoming increasingly difficult to make a living here."

Her stomach coiled itself into a burning knot. She knew her husband well enough to know he was setting the stage for something. Something big. Something she would not want to hear. She searched his deep blue eyes for meaning. Eyes that still captivated her heart and made it melt. "So, what exactly are you saying?"

"I'm saying that I myself have been thinking of leaving Sicily."

14

Like a bullet, Luca's words shot through her heart, reverberating with earthquake force in the depths of her soul. Her head began to spin as she grasped for understanding. "You can't mean that!" Surely she'd misheard her husband. He'd put all notions of going to America behind him when they'd married. They'd been through this before, and she had no intention of going through it again.

He looked at her.

What she saw in his eyes confirmed her worst fear.

"I mean it with all my heart."

Maria's stomach lodged in her throat. "But, Luca, our life is here. Your business is here. Our family is here." She turned her attention to her children. "What about the children? To uproot them would bring great hardship on them. A hardship that could ruin their futures."

Luca jumped in. "Or could *give* them a future."

Nico's face lit up. "Mama, I think it would be fun to move."

Precious Nico! What did he know about life at his tender young age? She still hadn't told him the truth about his birth father, Don Franco. She'd planned to do so the following year when Nico would turn twelve. "But what about your friends? Your school? Your taking over Papa's shop when you grow up?"

"I'll make new friends in a new school. As for taking over Papa's business, I can start my own tailor shop in America when I grow up."

Maria's body shook. "It isn't as easy as that, my son."

Luca intervened. "We can do all things through Christ Who gives us strength."

Bile rose to Maria's throat. "I don't need your quoting the Bible to me, Luca. I know that verse as well as you do."

"Then why don't you take it to heart, dear one?"

Why did Luca always have to be right? "But, Luca. Do you realize what going to America will do to our family? Do you realize what it will cost us?"

Her breath hitched. So much for her wonderful life!

Valeria began to cry, and Anna soon followed suit.

Maria rose from her place at the table to pick up her youngest child. "What's the matter, little one?"

The child buried her head in Maria's shoulder. "I'm scared."

Maria cradled Anna's head. "There's no need to be afraid."

Valeria climbed out of her chair and tugged on Maria's skirt. "I'm scared, too, Mama. Don't fight with Papa."

Stricken with guilt, Maria glanced at Luca. His eyes were riddled with pain. And Nico's troubled gaze cut her very heart.

She sat down and placed Anna on her lap. This was the first time her children had seen their parents argue. No wonder they were afraid.

Luca placed his hand on hers. "Look, Maria. Let's talk about this after dinner. Now is not the right time."

Her heart sank to the soles of her feet. As far as she was concerned, no time would ever be the right time.

Chapter Two

His stomach churning, Luca walked the dry fields of *Bella Terra* while Maria put the children to bed. A gentle breeze swept over the fields, causing the few remaining tomato plants to tremble in the hot and humid air.

It had not rained in weeks, and the crops lay dying under a cloudless sky. Luca's gaze followed the familiar hills in the distance, once covered with lush vineyards but now arid with thorns and thistles.

His heart sank. Sicily was dying. All around him, death reigned. In the fields. In the economy.

In the souls of his countrymen.

He and his family must leave before they, too, died.

A wild rabbit scurried across his path, searching for food. Even the animals were dying from lack of food.

Luca reached toward a withered green pepper plant, broke a piece of pepper off the vine, and tossed it toward the rabbit. The poor creature caught it and devoured it.

Dusk settled over the valley, shadowing it in a canopy of blues and purples. A swallow flitted across the sky, its soft chirping stirring the sorrow in Luca's heart.

Things had not gone well with Maria. Yet, her outburst of anger had not come as a surprise. Why would he have expected her to want to leave the land that had been her home since her birth? The land of her ancestors?

The land she'd fought so hard to save and restore?

He would have reacted the same way.

Yet, he hadn't told her the whole story. The other reason he felt called to America. The real reason.

Had he told her, it might have made a difference.

God had called him to preach the Gospel in America. To win souls for Him in a land that was prospering materially but dying spiritually.

He'd been sensing this call for a while now, but, like the Virgin Mary when the angel Gabriel announced she was with child, Luca had pondered this calling in his heart, wondering what it all meant. Trying to sort out its implications for his family.

Not revealing it to anyone until he was sure he'd heard from God. With each passing day, he'd grown more and more convinced that his destiny lay in the new world.

Yet, how could he follow God's call if Maria did not support him? He couldn't leave her and the children behind.

Could he?

Must he?

Others had left without their families to scout the new land before deciding whether or not to move their families there permanently. He could do the same.

But the very thought tore his insides apart. There was no way he could be separated from Maria for several months. Perhaps even years.

No. Either they would all go or they would all remain behind.

"Luca!"

The familiar voice interrupted his reverie. He turned to find Don Franco, his longtime friend, hurrying down the dirt path toward him. The former priest and schoolteacher—the man who, before his rebirth in Christ—had violently raped Maria. The man who'd experienced a powerful encounter with Christ. The man who'd been forgiven and was now foreman of *Bella Terra*. Don Franco smiled broadly. "Greetings!"

Luca extended a hand. "Franco, my friend. It is so good

to see you. How are you faring these days?"

"As well as can be expected, given the current situation in Sicily."

Luca nodded then frowned. "I heard you are leaving us. I am so sorry."

"You have heard correctly. I, too, am sorry. Extremely sorry. But with the economy fast collapsing, I had to consider my future. I will be taking a position as headmaster of a boarding school in Milano."

Luca nodded in approval. "Yes, Maria told me. That suits you far better than working the fields."

"Actually, the two are similar." Franco chuckled. "I will now be tending minds instead of plants."

Luca smiled. "And you will do a good job of it."

"Thank you." Franco grew serious. "So, what brings you out to the fields this evening?"

Luca studied Franco's kind face. "A concern heavy on my heart."

"Is everything all right?"

"Yes, as far as the family's health is concerned." Luca hesitated then went straight to the point. "Franco, I believe God is calling me to emigrate to America."

Franco raised an eyebrow. "That is, indeed, a heavy concern. Yet, at the same time an exciting one."

"I agree. But Maria doesn't want to leave *Bella Terra*. My business is not doing well. I must take action quickly, before the economy collapses completely and I am left without financial support for my family."

Luca hesitated. Should he share with Franco another even heavier concern? Luca's sense that God was calling him to preach the Gospel in America? A former priest would surely understand such a call.

Luca looked squarely at his longtime friend. "Franco, I have an even heavier concern."

19

Franco's gaze met Luca's.

"God has called me to preach the Gospel in America."

A knowing look crossed the priest's face. He smiled. "Yes, an even heavier concern, my friend. But a most joyful one."

"I agree. Serving the Lord always brings joy." Luca resumed his walking.

Franco fell into stride with him. "Have you told Maria of God's call?"

Luca shook his head. "No. I simply told her that my business is failing and that we must leave Sicily for better opportunities. Otherwise, we will go bankrupt."

"Perhaps if you tell her the real reason for your desire to leave, she will be more amenable. She has a heart for the things of God."

Luca considered Franco's words. Perhaps Luca had, indeed, been wrong in not telling Maria the greater reason for his desire to leave. He would do so that evening.

"Do you have connections in America?"

"I have only a former customer of mine—Giulio Genova—who lives in Brooklyn. He recently wrote saying that his boss was looking for good tailors and was offering me a job. I had been praying for direction, and Giulio's letter seemed to be a confirmation."

Franco nodded in agreement. "Yes, it seems so to me as well. Do you have any connections regarding the Gospel work to which God has called you?"

"Only the missionary who led me to the Lord. I have his name and the organization with which he was affiliated. The American Bible Society. I have nothing more. I have written to the organization requesting his whereabouts, but I have heard nothing yet."

"And if you do not?"

"I had not considered that eventuality." Luca searched

his heart. "If I do not hear anything, I will trust God and proceed anyway."

"That means you are convinced in your heart."

Luca smiled. "I suppose so."

"Then be persistent. If this calling is of God, He will lead you every step of the way."

Luca's muscles relaxed. "Thank you, Franco. I needed to hear those words to remind me that Jesus is the Good Shepherd and He leads His sheep."

Franco smiled. "Indeed, He does. And in ways we cannot fathom."

Luca nodded. "When will you be leaving?"

"A week from tomorrow. I will begin my duties as headmaster on the first of next month."

"You must have a meal with us before your departure."

"Thank you. I would love that."

Luca's eyes filled with tears as he studied the former priest's face, a face once filled with torment but now filled with peace because of the grace of God. Luca placed a hand on Franco's shoulder. "Franco, I will miss you. You have been a dear and precious friend these many years. May our Lord go with you as you follow the path He has carved out for you."

Tears welled up in Franco's eyes. "And with you, too, dear Luca." Franco's voice caught. "And please take good care of my Nico." As he uttered the words, he burst into tears.

A lump formed in Luca's throat. No words came. Only a tight, heart-wrenching embrace for the man standing before him.

* * * *

The children were sound asleep when Luca finally sat down with Maria at the kitchen table to talk about their future over a cup of espresso. Ever since he'd broken the news about America to her at dinner, she'd been distant. Worried.

Afraid.

He hoped their conversation would calm her fears.

Luca cleared his throat. "Maria, let me explain what I've been thinking."

"Very well, but I will tell you up front that I am not at all in agreement with you regarding this move." She clipped her words.

He placed a hand on hers. "Please don't be close-minded. Please give me a chance to explain first. Perhaps you will see things differently once I tell you the reason for my decision."

She withdrew her hand. "*Your* decision? Excuse me! Don't I have a say in the matter? After all, I'm *only* your wife." Her dark eyes flashed fire.

Luca squared his jaw. "Maria, please. Calm down. Just hear me out."

She crossed her arms tightly in front of her chest.

A shiver ran through Luca as he realized that, other than a few minor spats, this was the first major disagreement they'd had in their entire married life. Cold filled the pit of his stomach. What was happening to them? What was happening to the beautiful, loving relationship they'd had for five amazing years?

His heart sank. It was all his fault. Maybe this whole idea of moving to America was nonsense. Craziness.

Selfish ambition.

Luca took a sip of his coffee to give himself time to gather his thoughts. "Maria, listen. The economy in Sicily has been in a gradual decline for a long while. Fortunately, it hasn't affected us too much because I've had a steady flow of work, primarily from people leaving for America. But now that Italy has been defeated in its fight against Ethiopia, and now that the population is dwindling because of the mass exodus, so is the work. I can see it in the number of customers who come to my shop. That number has grown smaller and smaller." He lowered his gaze. "And so has our income."

She nodded. "What you say is true. I've noticed the same thing when I shop in the village. Every day the vendors and customers complain of rising prices and the failing economy. It's the number one topic of conversation. And I've had to stretch my food budget more and more."

Hopeful she'd come around, he leaned toward her. "And it's not going to get any better, darling. I'm concerned there will not be enough work left for me to support our family."

"But, surely, there will always be a need for tailors."

"Not if there are no people left to need a tailor." He placed his hand on hers. "Besides, people will make do with old clothes and will put off buying new ones when funds are low. Or they'll do any necessary alterations themselves."

She closed her eyes and shook her head as if to block out the truth.

Luca's heart sank.

She looked up. "But there must be another way to ensure our financial future without leaving Sicily. What about *Bella Terra*? We could live off its proceeds."

"Well, we're doing that now to some extent, although we have to split the profits with your mother and your sisters' families. Imagine what it will be like when my tailoring income drops to almost nothing. Our portion of the profits earned from *Bella Terra*'s produce would not be enough to support us."

"And what about Mama and my sisters? If we go to America, I may never see them again."

Luca tensed. "That possibility does, indeed, exist. I understand that."

She lifted her chin, her eyes aflame. "You really don't. Your parents are gone and you have no family here. You would be leaving behind only your homeland." Her voice caught. "I would be leaving behind my loved ones."

He could not deny the truth of what she'd said. "You are right, dear one. But if things go well for us, you could return frequently to visit them."

"But there's the big IF. What if things don't work out for us, Luca? What if we are about to make the biggest mistake of our lives?"

He fought the doubt her words stirred in his heart. Up until now, he'd been sure God had spoken to him. But what if he hadn't heard from God? What if he'd heard only the voice of his own selfish ambition? What if Maria were right and he were wrong? He'd be putting his family in a very dangerous position.

Her eyes narrowed. "When did you decide to move to America?"

"I've been thinking about it for a long while now. In fact, the Lord planted the desire in my heart before we were married, but the timing wasn't right."

She stood abruptly and placed her hands on her hips. Her gaze on him was fierce. "So, you lured me into marrying you, knowing that one day you'd thrust this on me and force me to leave my homeland?"

Luca's insides caved. "Maria, at the time I honestly thought I'd missed God's will regarding America. I thought the desire came from my own selfish ambitions. As I look back, I think the Lord was planting the seed for us to move one day, and now that seed has sprouted." He stood and took her in his arms. "You must believe me."

She resisted his embrace. "I do believe you. But I must admit that I feel betrayed."

Her words stunned him. "*Betrayed?*" He released her.

"Why? I never deceived you. I've always been perfectly honest with you."

"When you married me, were you still harboring the secret hope that one day you would go to America?"

He took both her hands. "No, Maria. When I married you, I was certain I had missed God and I belonged at your side." He turned from her, his shoulders sinking into his chest. "I never would have married you under false pretenses. I'm very sorry you would even think that of me."

She took him by the arm. "Oh, Luca, please forgive me. I can't believe I said such a horrible thing. I know you've never been false with me. It's my own fear that betrays me."

Luca drew her close. "I, too, am afraid."

She pulled back and studied his face. "Then why do you want to go?"

Luca looked squarely into her eyes. "Because I believe the Lord is commanding me to go. Not only to provide for my family, but for a far greater purpose." He hesitated. "I believe God is calling me to preach the Gospel in America. I cannot let fear stand in the way of the Lord's will."

Her face softened. "Are you absolutely sure?"

"As sure as I can possibly be."

She hesitated, her face revealing the intense struggle going on within her. "Luca, I do not want to go to America. If God is, indeed, calling you to do this, then He will have to show me Himself."

With that, she left the room, leaving Luca behind to swallow the thickness in his throat.

* * * *

Will Dempsey lifted his size-eleven, leather-boots-clad feet up onto his cluttered desk and leaned back in his rickety, wooden swivel chair. From his back fourth-floor office window, streaked with industrial fumes, his eyes gazed on the Brooklyn Bridge, a short distance from the rented tenement house workshop where he worked as chief foreman for the Oliver Cramdon Clothing Company. For the past eight years, the legendary bridge had provided the backdrop for Will's daily duties of hiring and overseeing the numerous immigrant tailors and seamstresses who would put money in his boss's pockets.

And, if Will played his cards right, a good chunk in his own.

He stared out at the pewter-gray sky, wishing he were anywhere else but here. Having to oversee dozens of Italians and Jews at the shop every day got under his skin. He hated all of them. If he didn't depend on them for his livelihood, he'd send them all back to where they came from.

And he'd give them a good reason never to return.

In the last few years, they'd entered the country in droves, bringing with them their ignorant ways, their poverty, and their faith.

It was the latter he hated the most. Only fools believed in God. A God he'd once believed in but whom he'd grown to hate and despise.

And, lately, even deny.

What had God ever done for him except take his wife and kid in a train wreck?

He wanted no part of a God like that.

He drew in a deep breath and turned away from the window toward the piles of papers awaiting his attention on his desk. The pile seemed to grow with each passing day, despite his efforts to whittle it down to size.

He stared at the dusty photograph of Katie and little Willie sitting on his desk. He'd taken it on their last outing to Coney Island, just before the accident. Despite the deep ache in his heart every time he looked at it, he couldn't put it away. He clung to it like a man clinging to a raft for dear life.

To let go would mean certain death.

He swallowed hard.

Better to forget by burying himself in his work.

And in the bottle.

He reached way back into his bottom desk drawer and pulled out the small flask of whiskey he kept hidden there. He unscrewed the cap and took a long swig. The smooth warmth of the liquor sliding down his throat invigorated him. Almost thirty years had passed since the famous Whiskey Wars in Brooklyn—tax-evasion disputes in which his own father had been indicted. But even now, the famous Irishtown ring—as Vinegar Hill, Brooklyn's Fifth Ward, was called—still teemed with moonshiners doing their best to evade tax laws and other discovery by the local and federal government.

He studied the schedule for the day. Nine o'clock: Meeting with his project manager, Giulio Genova, to discuss hiring a new tailor. Giulio had a friend coming in from Italy who needed a job.

Will shook his head. Despite his hatred for Italians and Jews, he couldn't deny they knew how to sew. In fact, they were masters at it. That was their only saving grace. Otherwise, he'd never allow them into his shop.

He glanced at his wristwatch. Eight-fifty-eight. He had two minutes to collect his thoughts.

He opened the top right drawer of his desk and took a Jensen & Wallach cigar from the cigar box he kept there. He prided himself on buying cigars from the biggest cigar-maker in Brooklyn. Biggest meant best, and Will wanted only the best.

He placed the cigar between his lips, lit the tip, and drew in a deep, satisfying draught of heavenly flavor.

A knock on the door brought him to attention. Must be Giulio.

27

"Come in."

Slowly the door opened, revealing a short, stocky man, with balding head and wearing a pair of clean, pressed overalls. "Good morning, Mr. Dempsey."

"Giulio, come in. I've been expecting you." Will motioned to a wooden chair opposite his desk. "Take a seat."

"Thank you." Cap in hand, Giulio sat down, remaining on the edge of the chair. "Thank you for taking the time to see me. I am most grateful."

Why did these Italians have to be so polite? It made hating them even harder.

"How are things going on the floor?" Giulio was one of his best workers and kept things running smoothly in the shop.

"Very well, Mr. Dempsey. Everyone is doing his job. As you know, there is plenty of work."

"Yes. And the harder we work, the more work there will be. As long as we keep Oliver Cramdon happy, he'll keep us happy." Will smiled, hoping Giulio would catch the meaning in his veiled threat.

From the anxious look on Giulio's face, Will had succeeded in getting his point across.

With his lower lip, Will shifted the half-smoked cigar that hung from his mouth, folded his hands on his ample abdomen, and turned toward Giulio. "So, tell me more about this Luca Tonetta guy. You say he's a terrific tailor?"

"Yes, Mr. Dempsey. An outstanding tailor. He is known all over Sicily for his fine work."

Will narrowed his eyes. These Italians all said the same thing about their friends in need of work. As if they didn't know Will could see right through them. "What proof do you have? Cramdon accepts no excuses when it comes to my hiring good help. He insists only on the best." Will pictured Oliver Cramdon, one of the biggest clothing manufacturers in the entire United States, shaking a warning finger at him to hire only the best. A no-nonsense man whose motto was, "Only the bottom-line. Give me only the bottom-line." Cramdon had made it very clear to Will that by bottom-line, he meant the profits he would pocket at the end of the day after all expenses were paid. If those profits were substantial, Will's cut would also be substantial. But a good bottom-line resulted only from good workmanship. Will had to be sure he hired only the best tailors. Otherwise, quality would suffer, and if quality suffered, profits would suffer.

Giulio's voice interrupted Will's mental tangent. "He was my personal tailor before I left Sicily and is known as one of the finest tailors in all of Sicily. He altered a couple of suits for me."

Dempsey eyed him squarely. "You know my reputation sits on whether or not what you're telling me is the truth."

Giulio nervously fingered his *coppola*. "I'm telling you the truth, Mr. Dempsey. I have no reason to lie to you."

Dempsey raised a thick eyebrow. "Don't you now? I know the way you Italians stick up for your buddies and paint them as better than they really are. You're masters at the art of exaggeration. I've dealt with enough of you by now to know the way you operate." He spat a piece of chewed up cigar into a nearby spittoon. "I wasn't born at night, Giulio. Especially not last night."

Giulio raised his right hand. "On my late father's grave—may he rest in peace—I'm telling you the truth, Mr. Dempsey."

Holding the stub of his cigar in his callused hands, Dempsey drew in a long draught then blew it out, filling the room with its pungent odor. "How soon can he get here?"

"Knowing Luca as I do, I am sure he will make arrangements to leave as soon as possible."

Dempsey nodded. "Good. That's real good. We've

already gotten some big orders that need to be ready in time for the Christmas retail season."

Giulio stood and shook Mr. Dempsey's hand. "Thank you, Mr. Dempsey! Thank you very much! You are a good man!"

"Don't speak too soon, Giulio. Mr. Tonetta—Luca— might have a different opinion of me when he sees what I demand of my workers." Will gave Giulio a warning look.

"I understand, Mr. Dempsey. I will alert Luca to your high expectations."

"No need to. I'll do that myself when he gets here."

Dempsey waved a dismissive hand toward Giulio. "Now, be on your way. There's a huge order to fill before closing time today. Get a move on!"

Giulio rose and gave Dempsey a slight bow. "As you say, Mr. Dempsey."

Dempsey laughed. "You got that right. *As I say.*"

Fidgeting with his cap, Giulio nodded and then left.

Will leaned back in his chair, his eyes on the door that Giulio had closed behind him. "And when his fellow Italian, Luca Tonetta, gets here," Will mumbled under his breath, "I'll see to it he gets it right, too."

Chapter Three

Maria tossed and turned in the large featherbed she shared with Luca. Despite the coolness of the night, beads of perspiration dotted her brow and dampened her hair. Her stomach churned and her head ached as she pondered her recent conversation with Luca. She'd walked out on their discussion—not a very Christ-like thing to do.

Guilt assailed her and sleep evaded her as her mind raced with fearful thoughts about Luca's desire to move to America. Why hadn't the Lord spoken to her as well? Surely He wouldn't speak only to Luca regarding such a major decision.

She examined her heart. Perhaps the Lord was speaking to her, too, but she wasn't listening.

Conviction settled over her spirit. Luca was a Godly man. He made no decision without prayer and deliberation. He counted the cost and considered the effects of his decisions on his family.

And he was willing to obey the Lord no matter what the price.

Yet, was she, like Luca, willing to pay the price of obedience? Was she willing to obey the Lord at all costs?

Was she willing to submit her will to the will of the Father?

The night sounds of *Bella Terra*, heretofore comforting and serene, now spoke of ending and loss. The shrill cry of a barn owl jangled her nerves and made every muscle in her body tense. Wherever she turned, once-welcome sounds and sights served only to fuel her grief at leaving the place she had called home for her entire life.

She lay on her back and stared at the ceiling. Through the open window, a cool and gentle breeze rustled the white lace curtains, billowing them into air-filled clouds of soft fabric. The sweet, honey-like fragrance of white alyssum filtered upward from the garden below, while the shrill and steady drilling of a choir of cicadas punctuated the otherwise peaceful night.

But her heart was not at peace. Instead, it pounded wildly as she contemplated the prospect of leaving *Bella Terra* for a foreign land. A land of promise, yes. But a land of unknown challenges as well. Would she be up to them? The very thought of leaving Mama and her sisters, of leaving her beloved *Bella Terra*, sickened her, suffocated her, threatening to throw her into utter despair.

She broke out in a cold sweat. Had Luca really heard from God? Or was this just a lustful lure for greener pastures? If so, how could she convince him to reconsider? Had he thought about the effect on the children? Uprooting young plants did not always result in fruitful growth once replanted in unfamiliar soil.

But when Luca made up his mind about something, there was no changing it. No convincing him otherwise.

No turning back.

Repositioning her pillow, she rolled over on her side. The first signs of dawn filtered through the billowing curtains, like pink and purple ribbons tying up the night sky. Yet, she hadn't slept a wink. While Luca slept soundly, thoughts of their earlier conversation strangled her sleep and robbed her of her peace. Every nerve in her body was on edge at the ominous prospect looming before her. Either she submitted to Luca's decision to move to America, or ….

Or what?

The only alternative was to remain behind. But that was

out of the question. She loved Luca and wanted to be by his side. And what about the children? They needed their father.

What if he went first to check out the territory? To make sure the reports he was hearing were true? Lots of husbands had done that. Of course, most had sent for their wives and children to follow them, but a few of the men had returned to Sicily. Maybe Luca would be one of them.

But her husband was determined to obey God at all costs. A good thing. But did obedience to God mean leaving behind everything she loved?

Dare she bargain with God? If He allowed them to remain at *Bella Terra*, she'd contribute more to the poor. She'd pray longer. She'd do whatever she had to do to hold on to the only life she knew—and wanted.

Foolish thoughts! No amount of doing good on her part could replace obedience to God. He'd said as much in His Word when He'd declared that obedience was better than sacrifice. Not only was the new birth made possible by grace alone, and not by works, so also was living out the Christian life made possible by grace alone, and not by works. So why was she trying to rationalize the truth?

O God, forgive me!

She rose and grabbed her robe from the chair on which she'd draped it the night before. Perhaps a cup of hot chamomile tea would settle the queasiness in her stomach and the uneasiness in her spirit.

As she made her way toward the kitchen, a rooster crowed in the distance, sending shivers down her spine.

The sound of betrayal.

The Apostle Peter had heard the same sound right after he'd betrayed Christ for the third time. Would refusing to go to America be an act of betrayal to the Lord she'd grown to love?

Conviction settled over her spirit as she remembered the

words of the Father in 1 Samuel 15: 22: *Behold, to obey is better than sacrifice, and to listen than the fat of rams.*

She poured some water into the teakettle and lit the stove. *Lord, I surrender to Your will. If going to America is Your will for us, then close all doors to remain in Sicily. Please make it clear to me, Lord.*

She listened intently for God's still, small voice within her.

But all she heard was silence.

* * * *

The morning after his argument with Maria, Luca arrived early at his shop. Nico remained behind to help the field hands with the harvest.

The day was hot and rainy, making Luca's walk to the village a muddy mess. But God knew they needed the rain. After nearly two months of drought, the earth of Pisano had reached the edges of death.

Even the large umbrella he carried had not been enough to keep the rain from splashing mud against his trousers. Good thing he kept a backup pair at the shop.

He plodded down the winding road toward the village, careful to avoid the numerous puddles that dotted the narrow dirt road. He could have taken the horse-drawn wagon, but he'd decided against it. Maintaining Bianca, his faithful old mare, cost money Luca no longer had. The more he drove her, the more he'd have to feed her and the more he'd have to spend on her upkeep. His heart tightened. If things didn't improve soon, he'd have to sell her.

He tilted the umbrella as the wind grew stronger. What had started out as a drizzle upon his departure had now turned into a driving rain. He quickened his pace toward the village.

A hollowness filled his chest as he approached the

square. His conversation with Maria the night before had not gone well. He'd lain awake for a long while before finally falling asleep, helplessly listening to her anguished weeping on the pillow beside him. This morning she'd seemed distant. Distracted.

Depressed.

He clenched his jaw. Should he even be thinking of going to America? Was the move worth putting his wife through such suffering?

Yet, what choice did he have if he wanted to support his family?

Sicily's economy was in shambles, and the future looked bleak. His business was failing, and any prospects of resurrecting it were slim, if not non-existent.

Worst of all, he was failing as a provider. A failure that, as far as he was concerned, ranked right up there with treason against one's country.

Luca swallowed the lump in his throat.

Pushing against the driving rain, he traversed the village square toward his shop. A few vendors had already arrived, optimistic that the weather would take a turn for the better, although on rainy days, many stayed home.

"Hey, Luca! Luca Tonetta!" Angelo the fish vendor greeted him with a broad smile. "Time to get out your rowboat." He laughed as rain washed over his stubbly face.

Luca returned the wave with a chuckle. "Sounds like a good idea, my friend."

As he approached the portico in front of his shop, Luca spotted a man sitting on the wooden bench just outside the door. As Luca drew closer, he recognized Silvestro, his landlord.

Luca's stomach tensed.

Silvestro sat, legs crossed, tapping his fingers on his knee. A scowl creased his rugged, sunburned face.

"Good morning, Silvestro." Luca moved under the shelter of the portico and closed his umbrella.

Silvestro stood to his full height. He was taller than Luca by about eight centimeters. An ugly scar lined his right cheek, the result of a brawl in which he'd been the loser.

"Not much good about it, I'd say." His voice was gruff, and his facial expression even more so. "I'm here to collect my back rent. You're two months overdue."

Luca's heart froze. He had only a few *lire* left, and he'd planned to buy food for his family with it. He collected his thoughts in a meager attempt to compose himself. "Let's go inside, please. Out of this rain."

Luca placed the wet umbrella under the bench and unlocked the front door. He motioned for Silvestro to enter before him.

Once they were both inside, Silvestro wasted no time in unleashing his venom. "I want my rent, and I want it now."

His heart pounding, Luca looked Silvestro squarely in the eye. "I do not have your rent. But I promise you I will do my best to get it to you before the end of the week."

Silvestro slammed a tight fist on the counter. "No! I've been patient with you long enough, Luca Tonetta. I have my own bills to pay and my own family to feed. I want no more of your lame excuses."

Luca sensed the fear underlying his anger. "Believe me, I understand."

Silvestro got in his face. His breath smelled of stale garlic. "The only thing you need to understand is that you owe me two months' rent and you'd better pay it now." His nostrils flared. "Or else I will evict you."

Luca took a step backward. "Silvestro, listen, please. I do not have the money to pay you now. But I will do my best to get it to you by the end of the week. You have my word."

The landlord's face turned a deep crimson. "Your word

means nothing to me. I want to see the *money*." He slammed his fist on the counter a second time. "And if I don't see the money by closing time today, I will evict you. Is that clear?"

Luca drew in a deep breath. No use arguing with an angry man. "As you say. You are the landlord."

Silvestro shook a crooked finger at him. "And don't you forget it! I will be back this afternoon for my money. If you don't have it by then, don't plan on coming back to your shop tomorrow morning, because it will no longer be yours." With that, he stormed out of the shop, slamming the door behind him.

Shoulders slumped, Luca sank onto the stool behind the counter. His insides roiled. Barring a miracle, there was no way he could earn enough money to pay his two months' back rent by the end of the work day.

He closed his eyes in prayer. "Father, if You want me to stay in Sicily, then bring the rent by the end of the day. If it does not come, then I will consider that a confirmation that You want me to take my family and move to America. I pray this in the Name of Jesus. Amen."

When Luca opened his eyes, he had a strong feeling the money would not be in his hands by the end of the day.

* * * *

By the time Luca left his shop for home that evening, the rain had subsided and the sun had peeked briefly through the clouds on its final descent to the horizon. Dusk followed close behind, bringing with it thick clouds in gray skies, portending more rain. A good thing, given the drought of the last two months. As if the weakened economy weren't bad enough, the drought served only to intensify Luca's thoughts about leaving Sicily.

Overhead, a seagull winged its way toward an unknown destination.

Luca drew in a deep breath of the salty sea air. As he'd sensed in his spirit while praying that morning, the rent money had not come in. On the contrary, the day's earnings had been next to nothing, with only one customer visiting his shop the entire day. The customer had asked for a minor alteration. Not even enough income for a single meal for his family.

With heavy heart and a lump in his throat, Luca locked the shop door behind him for the last time. At the sound of the key engaging the lock, he swallowed thickly. The shop in which his father had started the family business would now leave Luca's hands forever.

Gone were his dreams of bequeathing the shop to Nico. Of continuing his father's legacy through his son.

Of keeping the well-established Tonetta name alive in the tailoring trade of Sicily.

He stopped for a long moment, unwilling to release the doorknob as hot tears stung his eyes.

He was a failure.

A complete failure.

He'd failed his family.

He'd failed himself.

He'd even failed God.

He could no longer call himself a man.

Gazing one last time at the storefront sign that read *Tonetta's Tailoring*, he swallowed the lump that had lodged in his throat. As of the next morning, the shop would officially no longer be his. The shop where he'd grown up at his beloved father's side and learned the tailoring trade. The shop he'd taken over upon his father's untimely death.

The shop where he'd met Maria.

Precious memories filled its small rooms. Memories he would carry with him to his grave.

He suppressed the tears that stung his eyes.

He picked up the large knapsack into which he had thrown his meager belongings. His wooden cashbox, containing only a few *lire*. His sewing tools.

And his espresso coffee pot.

Earlier that day, Giacomo, the barber who rented the shop next door, had offered to transport Luca's sewing machine and desk to *Bella Terra* in his wagon. The two men had bid a tearful farewell to each other.

Luca thrust the knapsack over his right shoulder. Dark clouds rolled in from the east as he turned to face the shop one last time. His chest ached.

He adjusted the knapsack on his shoulder and headed toward the village square. All of the vendors had left for the day. Angelo the fish-vendor. Giuseppe the chicken farmer. Roberto the leather-worker. All good men.

And faithful friends.

He'd greeted them every morning for the last fifteen years, at least. They'd shared many a good meal and many a good laugh, and borne one another's burdens. How he would miss them!

A light wind brushed Luca's face, carrying with it the sweet fragrance of the purple bougainvillea that struggled for life at the edge of the square. Shoving his hands deep into his pockets, he made his way across the square, past the ornate marble fountain in the center, toward the road leading up the hillside to *Bella Terra*. The short stretch of afternoon sun had dried the puddles, leaving behind a network of potholes in the road. He deftly avoided them.

He gazed around him. This would be the last time he'd make the trip up this hill on his way home from work. The last time he'd look forward to coming home to Maria and the children after a long day of tailoring.

The last time he'd experience the beauty of the hills surrounding Pisano.

He tensed. What would Maria say when she heard that Silvestro had evicted him? Would she be angry? Disappointed? Afraid?

Probably all three.

She'd married him *"for better or worse,"* but he certainly hadn't planned on giving her "worse." Yet, a spark of hope remained if they would only go to America. Maybe his loss of the shop would convince her that leaving Sicily was God's will for them.

The only way for them to survive.

He rounded the final bend in the road that led to Maria's beautiful family villa called *Bella Terra.* The home he'd made his own ever since their marriage five years earlier. Despite its urgent need of repair, it still sat at the top of the hill like a queen, regal and majestic on the highest elevation overlooking the valley. No wonder Maria loved her so. Throughout her two centuries, the villa had seen much. Had anyone else in Maria's family had to leave her for a better life? Would she be the first one to leave in defeat?

All because of him.

Luca clenched his fists.

As he approached the back veranda, the aroma of garlic and olive oil wafted through the open kitchen window. Maria was preparing the evening meal. How would she receive him after their argument?

His stomach in a tight knot, he entered through the back door and stopped.

Maria's gaze met his. Her eyes told him she knew.

He remained standing, facing his wife. "I've been evicted."

Chapter Four

Will Dempsey entered the large workshop where the twenty-eight employees he supervised worked feverishly to fill orders for Brooklyn's biggest clothing manufacturer, Oliver Cramdon, Ltd. Will prided himself on having landed the contract that was the envy of all the garment workshops in the borough and beyond, and he had been the lucky one to win it. Of course, a little finagling here and there hadn't hurt the effort. A guy had to do what he had to do, right?

He pushed aside the slight twinge of guilt that still managed to prick his conscience. A conscience that, since the death of Katie and their only child, had grown hard and callus. Why should Will care when God didn't? Had God cared, He wouldn't have taken Will's only two reasons for living.

He swallowed the burning ache that never died.

Losing Katie and the kid was bad enough. But losing Katie also meant losing his chief cook and bottle-washer. Katie had been his right-hand man.

Or woman.

She'd run the home and taken care of keeping things in order. After she died, he'd had to hire a cook to take over the job.

More money out of his pocket.

Not to mention meals that weren't fit for a dog.

"Good morning, Mr. Dempsey." Jake Goldberg smiled from behind his sewing machine and waved. Jake was one of Will's best tailors. He rode a sewing machine with the expertise of a jockey riding a champion racehorse. Jake was a faithful worker, although his constant smile annoyed Will to no end. How could a guy be happy working in these conditions?

Will waved in return. "Mornin', Jake. A shipment of piece cuts will be comin' in this afternoon. Be sure you take care of distributing them to the right people."

"Do not worry, Mr. Dempsey. Jake is your man."

Jake was his man all right. If only he weren't a Jew.

But it wasn't only the Jews who irritated Will. The Italians were even worse. If he had his druthers, he'd hire only Americans for the job. People who'd been here for a few generations. But they weren't willing to put up with low wages and uncomfortable working conditions. Besides, immigrant labor was cheap, and he could squeeze them to the very last drop. The harder he worked them, the more money he could stuff into his pockets at the end of the day.

And the more he stuffed into his pockets, the more he could drown out his sorrows in good ol' Irish whiskey at O'Malley's Tavern.

Will walked down the aisle alongside the rows of rectangular worktables. Each one seated four workers, two on each side. The first section held the basters who prepared the garments by fitting the pieces together. These fitted pieces would then be passed to the sewing machine operators who sewed them into the finished garment. Once sewn together, the sewing machine operators would pass the product to the finishers for the final touches that were applied by hand. After that, the garments went to the presser who ironed them and made them ready for the retail stores.

Will had two pressers, both elderly men with muscles strong enough to lift the twenty-pound irons. And both Orthodox Jews.

Whatever Will disliked about the Italians and the Jews, he had to concede they were good workers.

Not so, the other immigrants. Some were good; some not so good.

Like Paulina Ivanov.

If he had to reprimand her one more time for being late, would he have the courage to fire her?

She gave him a smile and a sidelong glance as he passed by. "Good morning, Mr. Dempsey." She batted her long, dark eyelashes.

She wasn't bad-looking as far as women went. A little on the plump side, but not unpleasantly so. But her flirtatious conduct bordered on the immoral. He wondered why he'd ever hired her, except for the fact she was an outstanding finisher, and he'd needed one badly.

He nodded. "Good morning." His reply was curt as he started to move toward the next table.

She rose and came around to him, her hands clasped together. "Mr. Dempsey, I have a favor to ask of you."

He stopped and faced her.

She reached his chin in height. Had she not been wearing high heels, she'd be no taller than his shoulder.

She gave him her best smile. "May I have off next Saturday? My sister is getting married."

Will looked her in the eye. Was she telling the truth? He'd been in the business long enough to name every excuse in the book for getting a day off.

"Is that so?" He studied her lovely face, looking for a sign of deception.

"Yes. I am the maid of honor." Her soft Russian accent gave a musical quality to the English words, slightly disarming him.

"What if I said no?"

Her eyes widened in surprise. "I had not even considered you would say no."

"Then why did you ask me? Why didn't you just tell

me?"

Will was giving her a hard time and he knew it. Not only knew it, but enjoyed it.

"That would have been disrespectful."

He put his hands on his hips. "Okay, you can have the day off. But you'll have to make the time up on another weekend. Christmas orders are coming in already, and I need all the help I can get."

"Of course, Mr. Dempsey." She flashed a smile. "I will even work two Saturdays for you to make up for this one."

He smiled at her spunk.

And at her negotiating skills.

"So, you're the maid of honor, huh?"

A frown crossed her face. "Yes. But I would much prefer to be the bride."

Something about the way she said it gave him pause. "Your turn will come, Paulina. Your turn will come."

She lowered her eyes and then looked up at him. "Do you really think so, Mr. Dempsey?"

Her forlorn look tugged at his heart.

"I not only think so; I *know* so."

* * * *

Maria's heart lurched at the sight of Luca's face. It was pale and drawn.

He looked at her but did not smile.

She wiped her hands on a kitchen towel, approached him, and took him by the arms. "What happened?" She was glad Nico was outside playing and Mama had taken the little ones for the afternoon. She and Luca could talk privately.

"Silvestro came this morning demanding payment of two months' of my back rent. I didn't have it. He gave me till the end of the day to come up with the money, but I was unable to."

A cold chill gripped Maria's stomach. "So what does this mean?"

"It means I've lost my business."

He moved toward the kitchen table and sat down, leaning his forehead against the palm of his hand.

Maria sat down next to him. "But surely you can find another place to rent?"

He looked at her in disbelief. "Maria, if I don't have enough money to pay rent to Silvestro, what makes you think I'll have enough money to pay rent to someone else?"

Her heart caught in her throat. Luca was right. What was she thinking? "Can you use a room here at *Bella Terra* as your workshop?"

He shook his head. "Customers aren't going to travel all the way to *Bella Terra* to do business. Besides, it would only add to my expenses to have my supplies delivered the extra distance. I need a place in the center of the village, easily accessible to customers and suppliers alike."

She placed a hand on his. "So, what are we going to do?"

Before he replied, she already knew the answer in her heart. There was nothing else to do but go to America.

Remember, dear one, you asked Me for a sign? A very specific one? That I would close all doors for you to remain in Sicily?

Her heart sank. Yes, she'd asked the Lord for a sign, and she'd gotten the very one she'd asked for but had hoped not to get.

Luca lifted his eyes toward her. They were pure and full of love. "Maria, I think we have no choice but to go to America. Trying to continue my business in an economy that is collapsing and a country that is dying is foolishness. God has provided a land where we can not only survive, but also thrive." He took her hand. "I think God is making His will for us quite clear."

She swallowed hard. "I think you are right." She forced a smile.

Color returned to Luca's ashen face. Her words had restored his soul, and she was glad.

The hint of a smile broke across his face. "So, you are in agreement? We can begin making plans to move soon?"

As much as it pained her to admit it, she agreed. "Yes, we can begin making plans to move." Even as she spoke the words, her heart wept. Moving to America meant leaving behind all that she'd ever known, ever loved, ever hoped for. It wasn't going to be easy.

But because she loved God and her husband, she could do nothing less than to obey.

"I must tell Mama right away."

"And I will confirm our decision with Giulio right away." Luca rose and took both her hands, drawing her up toward him. "You have no idea what it means to me to have you on my side and by my side." He cradled her head in his shoulder. "I want nothing more than the best for you and the children." He stroked her long, silky hair. "And I promise you I will do my best to provide for you in every way."

He kissed her just as Mama entered the kitchen with the children.

"I thought you were supposed to be cooking," Mama joked.

The children rushed toward Luca. "Papa! Papa! We planted sunflowers with *Nonna* today!"

Luca gathered his children into his arms, his face hopeful once again. "What fun! When will they bloom?"

Valeria shouted first. "In three months!"

Maria's breath caught. *Just in time for their departure to America.* Maria turned to Mama. "Mama, Luca and I have something very important to tell you."

Mama's eyes widened. "You are expecting another child?"

Maria laughed in spite of herself. Italian *nonnas* were always looking to add more grandchildren to their grandmotherly crown of human jewels. Maria had often overheard her mother bragging to her friends about the number of grandchildren she had. Precious feathers in her generational cap. Indeed, an unspoken competition existed among the village grandmothers for first place in the number of one's progeny. And the competition could get fierce.

Maria took a deep breath. Would that the matter were simply one of another grandchild on the way! Instead, the reality was that her mother would be parting with her only three grandchildren, not to mention her eldest daughter, for an indefinite period of time.

Perhaps forever.

Maria swallowed hard. "Mama, I wish what I had to tell you were the good news of another grandchild. But I'm afraid it is not such happy news." In a rush of anguish, she blurted out the words. "Luca, the children, and I will be moving to America."

Mama's face blanched as her eyes registered disbelief. She threw her hands to her pallid cheeks and shook her head. "But this cannot be!" She turned toward Luca. "Surely, you would not take my grandchildren from me. And you would not deprive me of my firstborn child." The elderly woman wrung her hands.

Luca cleared his throat. "I know this is difficult for you, but I truly believe I have heard from the Lord, and, because I love Him, I have no choice but to obey His voice. To do otherwise would be to deny Him."

Mama's eyes pleaded. "But could you not go ahead of Maria and the children to check out the situation first? It's possible that it will not be what you expect and that you will decide to return to Sicily."

"Yes, I could go on ahead. Maria and I have even considered that option. But after much discussion, she has decided to go with me."

Mama shook her head from side to side as tears spilled on to her wrinkled cheeks. "I am old. I may never see my daughter and grandchildren again."

Maria's heart clenched as she studied her mother's anguished face. A face she'd grown to love and cherish for almost thirty years. What if her mother were right? What if going to America meant they would never see each other again? What if Mama died without ever seeing Nico, Valeria, and Anna again?

Her heart breaking, Maria rose and placed her hands on her mother's frail shoulders. So frail Maria could feel the fragile bones beneath her fingers. "Don't worry, Mama. I will write to you and keep you abreast of all that is happening." The words caught in her throat and dissipated into a thin, choking whisper. "I promise you."

Her mother took a white handkerchief from her apron pocket and dabbed her eyes. "If this is the Lord's will, who am I to stand in His way?" The elderly woman rose and drew Maria into a tight embrace that ripped Maria's heart in two. For a long moment, Mama held her, as though letting go of her daughter would cause her to disappear. Then, drawing back, Mama ran a trembling hand over Maria's cheek. "So, when will you leave?"

"In early September."

Mama lowered her eyes then raised them again, her face contorted with anguish. "May God go with you, my child." She then turned toward her grandchildren seated at the table. "And with my grand—."

But before the words had completely left her tongue, she burst into tears and left the room.

Maria's gaze followed after her. *Lord, please let the sunflowers bloom before we leave.*

* * * *

That evening, Luca sat at the kitchen table to write to Giulio, confirming his acceptance of Mr. Dempsey's job offer. Maria busily cleaned up the kitchen while Valeria and Anna played at her feet.

Luca would book passage for them the next day, making sure to arrive in time to begin work on October 1st. He would notify Giulio later of the exact date of their arrival in New York.

Luca dipped his quill pen into the inkwell once again and signed his name to the letter. He then folded it, inscribed Giulio's address on the front, and sealed it with hot wax in preparation for mailing. Tomorrow morning he would take the letter to the post office and make arrangements for their departure.

"Papa, Papa, look!" Nico entered the kitchen, his furry *Lagotto Romagnolo* puppy at his side. "Pippo, show Papa how you prance."

Valeria and Anna looked up from their play and giggled as Nico demonstrated Pippo's latest trick.

"Prance, Pippo! Prance like a man!"

The fluffy, brown-and-white creature followed Nico around the kitchen on his hind legs while the little girls clapped their hands in delight.

Valeria shouted at the top of her lungs. "Mama, Pippo is walking like a person!"

Luca watched with delight as his son gave his canine companion a big hug. A gift from Nico's grandmother on his eleventh birthday, Pippo had wended his way into Nico's young heart with a charm that never ceased to delight him. In the short time the pup had belonged to the boy, they'd become best buddies. Inseparable. And in tune with each other like two instruments in an orchestra.

The little dog barked, his tail wagging at top speed.

"Guess what, Pippo?" Nico patted the puppy's head. "We're going to America! And you're coming with us!"

Pippo tilted his head as if to question where America was.

Luca's heart caught in his throat. How would he tell his son that Pippo could not come to America? That pets were not permitted on immigrant ships?

That they would have to leave the puppy behind?

Nico picked up the pup and nuzzled him under his chin. "America is far away, Pippo, across the big Atlantic Ocean. But I know we both will like it there." Nico smiled as the dog licked his face. "Papa says America is the new Promised Land, a place where we can have a better life."

Pippo barked in response, his tail wagging.

Nico laughed. "I knew you would agree." He patted the dog once again.

Luca could contain himself no longer. "I'm afraid Pippo cannot come with us, son."

Nico's face paled. "What do you mean, Papa? Why can't Pippo come with us? Surely, there are dogs in America."

Luca's heart filled with compassion. "Yes, I'm sure there are many dogs in America. But pets are not permitted onboard the ship. Besides, taking Pippo with us will hamper us in many ways, not the least of which is in our living arrangements. We will not have a large area in which Pippo can run around. At least, not at first. Brooklyn is not like the wide-open countryside we have here in Pisano."

Nico bit his lip as his eyes welled up with tears. "Then I can't go with you, Papa. I can't leave Pippo behind. Who will take care of him?"

"We can leave him here with *Nonna*, *Zia* Luciana, and

Zia Cristina. Pippo knows them well. I'm sure they will take good care of him."

"But I can't leave him behind, Papa! Don't you understand? I just can't. I'm the only master Pippo has ever known. He will be so sad and lonely without me." A sob spilled from the boy's voice. "He might even die!"

Luca reached for his son. "All you are saying is true. But when God calls us to do something for Him, we must obey, no matter what the cost."

Nico stiffened and pulled away, a scowl covering his face. "I know we must obey God, Papa, but why won't God let me take Pippo with me? He knows how much I love him."

Luca placed his hands on Nico's shoulders. "It is not God Who is keeping you from taking Pippo with you. It is the restrictions of the sailing line. We must abide by their rules."

"But it's not fair, Papa. Pippo wouldn't do any harm. He's a good dog. He would make the trip fun."

Luca's heart ached for his son, but he could not violate the rules. "I'm sorry, son. There is no way we can take Pippo with us. The ship line will not allow it. Besides, we have too much to think about without worrying about a dog."

"But Pippo isn't just any dog, Papa. He's a part of our family. I won't leave him behind."

Luca grew stern. "Nico, the matter is settled. We are not taking Pippo with us."

His lower lip quivering, Nico folded his arms tightly across his chest. "Then I'm not going with you, either. If you leave Pippo behind, you will have to leave me behind as well. I refuse to be separated from him."

Luca drew in a deep breath. The boy's heart was breaking. Becoming demanding would not do any good. Nor was it in Luca's nature to act in such a manner. Despite his mandate, his heart ached for his son. "Then you can remain behind with *Nonna* and your aunts, if you'd prefer."

Maria raised a palm in protest. "No, I will not allow that."

Nico's eyes widened in surprise. "Why not, Mama?"

"I want us to stay together as a family. Besides, I would miss you terribly."

Nico lowered his eyes. "I'll come for your sake, Mama." His voice was resigned. "But I will never forgive Papa."

With heavy heart, Luca resumed his letter-writing. But a single question bombarded his mind: Would the price of obeying God cost him his relationship with his son?

Chapter Five

A fast-setting sun cast long shadows over Will's desk as he finished typing the work contract for Luca Tonetta. Giulio had informed Will that Luca had accepted his job offer and would begin work October 1st. Almost three months away.

Will leaned his forehead on his palm. Luca's acceptance of the job had taken a load off Will's mind. A heavy load.

The big boss was already breathing down his neck to make this Christmas season the most profitable yet. But to do that, Will needed workers.

Good workers.

Despite his intense dislike for Italians, they were usually pretty skilled producers. From what Giulio said, Luca was topnotch.

Will sighed. Giulio had better be right. But only time would tell.

Will tugged the sheet of paper out of the typewriter roller and placed it on his desk. He re-read the contract to make sure there were no mistakes. Satisfied that it was correct, he signed it and put it in the top right-hand drawer of his desk to await Luca's arrival.

Will leaned back in his old swivel chair and turned it toward the grimy window that overlooked the Brooklyn Bridge and the East River. It'd been a long, hot day. One of the worst in Brooklyn's history. Even with every window in the place open, the heat had been stifling.

He squared his jaw as that same loneliness that hit him in the chest every night after work hit him again. The burning pain of having no one to go home to sliced his soul. There was the emptiness again. Right on schedule.

Would it ever stop showing up?

He rose to shut his window before leaving for the day. The smell of diesel fuel from the Coney Island elevated train filled his nasal passages, reminding him of the fortunate ones heading to Coney Island Beach on this hot summer day.

Will swallowed the lump in his throat. His wife and kid had loved the beach. Every summer weekend, when they were alive, he'd take them to Coney Island. They'd leave on Friday night after work, have a bite to eat, and then play the arcades. They'd stay in a cheap hotel and spend all day Saturday lying on the beach. On Saturday nights, they'd take the El home to their flat in Bensonhurst.

But those days were gone.

Gone forever.

Will secured the window latch, pulled on the long draw-string to turn off the single light bulb hanging from the ceiling, and closed the door behind him.

The building was quiet. Everyone had gone home for the weekend. Home to the loved ones for whom they'd worked hard all week.

Whom did he have to work for?

Himself?

There was no enjoyment in that.

Oh, maybe just a little in the whiskey he drank at O'Malley's Tavern nearly every night. Or in the young wench he'd find looking for a shoulder to cry on.

Or in the expensive cigars with which he regaled himself.

He hurried down the long flight of stairs to the ground floor, exited the building, and turned right toward O'Malley's. At least there, Brian O'Malley was waiting for him.

Waiting to listen yet again to his old jokes. Waiting to

help him drown his sorrow in one of the many O'Malley weekend specials.

Waiting to separate Will from his hard-earned money.

Katie and the kid flashed before his eyes. His heart twisted. He still thought he saw them in the crowds hurrying by. Once he'd stopped a woman and her boy to double-check. She'd scowled at him, grabbed her little boy's hand, and hurried away.

Will cringed at the memory and quickened his step. Better to drown his sorrow than to carry it. Better to forget than to remember.

Better to die than to live.

* * * *

Early morning light filtered through the open bedroom window and floated in on the fragrance of late summer roses. Maria took a deep breath, pressed down the lid of the large trunk, and latched it shut. At last, they were all packed and ready to go. Tomorrow morning, she, Luca, and the children would take the first train to Palermo at dawn, accompanied by Mama, Luciana, Cristina, and brother-in-law Pietro who insisted on seeing them off at the seaport. At two o'clock in the afternoon, Luca, Maria, and the children would board the *Argentina*, the large passenger ship that would carry them across the seas to their new life in America.

The past two months had been a whirlwind of activity in preparation for their departure. Now the dreaded day was at hand, and there was no turning back.

Maria sighed. Only God knew what lay ahead. Despite her reluctance to go, she would trust Him to watch over them.

Tears welled up in her eyes as she scanned the bedroom that had been hers ever since she was a child of two years old. She'd memorized the room's every crack, from the long, crooked one that ran across the ceiling directly above the large oaken dresser to the straight one that slid down the beige stucco wall opposite her bed. What fun she'd had as a child imagining she was sliding down the wall on that very crack! When she hit bottom, she'd mentally retrace her climb and slide down all over again.

Memories flooded her mind. Beautiful memories of childhood days spent working in the fields beside Papa. Of summer nights lying on the grass and watching the stars twinkle against a velvet indigo sky. Of lazy afternoons looking for animal shapes in the white cumulus clouds overhead. Of family picnics on rolling hillside meadows bursting with bright yellow sorrel and tiny blue iris wildflowers. If she closed her eyes, she could still smell the fragrance of almond blossoms against her cheek as she picked two small bunches, one to adorn her long braids and the other to take to Mama.

A lump formed in her throat. Those had been happy days. Carefree days. Days of childlike wonder and hope.

Days that knew no sorrow or the prospect of change.

Days that were gone forever.

She wiped a tear from her eye. Then, as she did when she was a little girl, she took off her shoes and walked barefoot across the ancient, knotted hardwood floor that had supported the feet of four generations of Landros before her. Had its coolness refreshed the soles of their feet as it had refreshed hers? Was she betraying their legacy by leaving? Was she surrendering the family torch entrusted to her by the faithful ones who had gone before her?

Worst of all, was she robbing her children of a future that rightfully belonged to them?

Her chest ached. She walked to the casement window that overlooked the fields ready for harvest. *Bella Terra*'s few remaining hired hands dotted the landscape, each bent over under a hot sun to bring in the harvest. A harvest that would be meager this year.

Maria crossed her arms and hugged her shoulders. What would Papa think of her leaving *Bella Terra* for a better land? She smiled through hot tears rolling down her cheeks. It was a moot question. Papa would say there was no better land than *Bella Terra*.

In her heart of hearts, she agreed.

If only Papa were still alive. Maybe he could convince Luca to stay.

The sound of footsteps interrupted her reverie. She turned to find Luca standing behind her.

His eyes registered compassion and anticipation. "Is the trunk ready for me to carry downstairs?"

She smiled faintly. "Yes. I've finished packing. I think we're ready to leave."

He took her in his arms. "Maria, thank you for agreeing to go with me. I know how difficult this is for you."

Her heart sank. He really *didn't* know. He hadn't been born on *Bella Terra*. Hadn't grown up here.

Hadn't intertwined his heart with the land.

Yet, he had lived here for five years and grown to love it.

She swallowed the lump in her throat and melted into the security of his embrace.

He pressed his lips against her forehead. "I promise you that if things don't work out in America, we'll return to Sicily."

Hope stirred within her. She looked up at him, searching his eyes. "Do you really mean that?"

He tucked a rebellious strand of hair behind her ear. "Have I ever broken a promise I've made to you?"

She shook her head. "No." She looked deep into his eyes. Eyes that were clear and pure and true. "And I know you never will."

He kissed her. "Come now. I'll carry this trunk down to the kitchen. Salvatore will be here early tomorrow morning to load the wagon."

Maria followed Luca to the kitchen and then went outside for one last walk in the garden. As her eyes drank in its natural beauty, her heart suddenly burst with joy.

The sunflowers had bloomed!

* * * *

On the day of their departure, Luca rose long before dawn. He'd planned to leave early to allow for any unforeseen events along the way to Palermo. The train trip would take about three hours, giving them an additional four-hour margin of time before they would board the *Argentina* and set sail for America at two o'clock that afternoon.

Maria's mother, Maria's sisters Luciana and Cristina, and Cristina's husband Pietro would be accompanying them on the train to Palermo. Despite Luca's advice against their making the trip, they'd insisted on bidding them farewell at the port. Luca hoped it wouldn't be too much of a strain on Maria's mother, who was frail and unwell.

Careful not to awaken Maria, he washed and dressed quickly. Then he went out to the back veranda to meet Salvatore. Their old and faithful farmhand had offered to help Luca load the wagon in preparation for their journey and then drive them to the train station in Ribera. The train was scheduled to leave at seven o'clock a.m. They would need to be on the road by six o'clock a.m.

The morning air was brisk as Luca pushed through the back door that led from the kitchen to the veranda. A waning moon hung low over the distant hills, giving place to the gently stretching fingers of an awakening dawn. A scarlet-bellied mountain tanager sat on a nearby beech tree, trilling a cheerful welcome to the new day.

Luca's heart stirred. The long-awaited day of their departure had finally arrived. Was this really happening? Was he really leaving his beloved Sicily, or was this all a dream?

He took a long breath of the fresh air of *Bella Terra*, wanting to savor its familiar scent one last time. For the past five years, since his marriage to Maria, this had been his home. He'd grown to love and appreciate its unique personality and the magnificent beauty of its surrounding countryside. *Bella Terra* had penetrated his soul and become an inextricable part of it. No wonder Maria hated so much to leave it.

As his memory photographed the landscape, a sense of finality enveloped him. Although he planned to return one day with Maria and the children, at least for a visit, would he ever do so? Or would life's path keep him forever from returning to his native land?

Only God knew. And only time would tell. But, just in case this was the last time he would tread the precious soil of *Bella Terra*, he wanted to engrave the memory of this place he called home indelibly on his heart. Its earthy smells. Its peaceful sounds. The feel of the lush soil running through his fingers. The sight of the rolling hills, purple and brown under the sun's warm rays.

His gaze drifted beyond the distant hills. What lay in the future? What would become of them in the new world? Was he doing the right thing uprooting his family from all they knew?

He raked his fingers through his hair. His goal was to work hard in their new homeland to provide a decent life for his family. He would do whatever it took to ensure their financial security. Otherwise, he could not call himself a man.

His stomach tightened. But what if things didn't work out the way he hoped? What if he failed?

What if he were leading his family into a situation far worse than the one they were leaving?

A rooster crowed, ushering in the new day. And a shiver of doubt coursed through Luca's soul.

He harnessed his straying thoughts. He must remain focused on his goal, focused on his purpose.

Focused on his God.

Only in this way could he accomplish the mission set before him. A mission not only to ensure a better life for his family, but also to proclaim the Gospel in his new homeland.

Luca found Salvatore sitting on the back porch stoop. "Good morning, my friend."

Salvatore rose, his worn *coppola* hat dangling from his callused fingers. Years of tilling the soil had left his back bent and his shoulders curved. "Good morning, *Signor* Luca. It looks like a good day to travel."

Luca looked up at the sky. The first pastel colors of dawn traced the horizon, blending the dark blue of night into brightening shades of pink and purple. "Indeed, it does. Praise the Lord!" Luca placed a hand on Salvatore's shoulder. "Thank you for getting up so early to help me."

"I am happy to help you. In truth, it is no sacrifice for me as I am up with the roosters every day."

Luca laughed. "There is something special about getting up with the roosters. It gives one a clearer perspective on life. Time alone with God before the responsibilities of the day crowd in."

Salvatore nodded. "Yes. A much better start on the day ahead."

Luca sighed. "Although, I must confess, I didn't have much time for that this morning. Not a good thing."

Luca pointed toward the house. "The trunk is in the

kitchen. I carried it downstairs last night. There are also two large suitcases to load and a large wicker basket that Maria has filled with food."

"Very well."

Luca placed a hand on Salvatore's shoulder. "Let's go. Two of us together will make light work of it."

Luca led the way to the kitchen. The large trunk sat by the door. Luca had wrapped two sturdy cords of thick rope around it for added security against its breaking open. Maria had packed it to the utmost.

He turned to Salvatore. "Are you ready, my friend?"

Salvatore laughed. "Ready as a cat about to pounce on a mouse."

Luca returned the laugh. "Well, this is no mouse, I can assure you."

Luca took one end of the trunk while Salvatore took the other. Hoisting it upward from the floor and onto his right shoulder, Luca led the way out the door. Proceeding slowly, he gauged Salvatore's pace and kept in step with it.

The wagon was only a few yards away. Turning the trunk horizontally so as to face the back of the wagon, Luca gently began to lower it into the wagon, with Salvatore following suit.

Luca heaved a sigh. "I think Maria packed everything we own in this trunk."

Salvatore laughed. "Women want to be sure they have everything they need to run a household properly. My wife is the same way. In fact, she'd probably take two trunks."

Just then, Maria appeared at the doorway, her face ashen, her lips trembling. "Luca, I cannot find Nico."

Luca froze. "What do you mean? He's asleep in bed."

"No. I went to waken him but he was not in bed. Nor was Pippo lying on the rug beside him as he always does."

"Perhaps Nico is in the outhouse. Did you check there?"

"I've checked everywhere. He is nowhere to be found I tell you. I'm frantic with worry."

Luca deposited the trunk on the wagon bed. He shook his head, his muscles tightening throughout his body. "This is so unlike Nico. Something must have happened to upset him."

Maria swept a hand across her forehead. "He's upset about Pippo, I tell you. He doesn't want to leave his dog behind."

Luca strode toward her. "But I thought that whole issue was settled."

"Apparently, it wasn't. Luca, we must find him!" She wrung her hands. "I will not leave without him."

"But our train leaves in two hours, and our ship at two o'clock this afternoon."

"There is no way I will leave without Nico." Maria's voice was firm. "I won't do it!"

Truth be told, neither would Luca.

He scrubbed a hand over his face and turned to Salvatore. "Thank you for your help."

"*Signor* Luca, please, let me help you search for Nico. I know *Bella Terra* like the back of my hand."

"It's really not necessary. I'm sure the boy will turn up soon." Luca hesitated, his limbs shaking, his soul even more so. "Of course, we would appreciate the extra pair of eyes. Especially since time is running short."

"Of course."

Luca divided the labor. "Salvatore, you search the barn and the workers' quarters since you know them well. I'll search the fields and the hillsides. Maria, you look through the house again and keep an eye on the younger children. I don't want them running off, too, in search of their brother. We'll meet back here to report in thirty minutes. Not one minute more."

Luca left abruptly and headed toward the wide-open fields surrounding *Bella Terra*. With trembling heart, he dug his nails into his hands at this unexpected turn of events. Nico was not a child to run away or rebel. Nor was he one to leave without saying where he was going. He had always been obedient and respectful. Only something extremely upsetting to him could have caused him to act in such an irrational manner. To disappear without warning. The boy knew they had to leave. Something dreadful must have happened to cause him to disappear.

Luca's throat grew thick. Maria must be right. Nico's disappearance had to do with his dog Pippo. The boy could not bring himself to leave his beloved pet.

But why did Nico have to wait until the last minute to run away? Why could he not have done so when they had more time to look for him?

Luca's cheeks burned at the shameful thought. How could he think of himself when the boy's very life might be in danger?

Luca followed the winding, dirt path that led to the main fields of *Bella Terra*. The morning was already growing warm with the oppressive humidity of late summer. A thick haze lay heavy like a low cloud over the countryside, portending a very hot day. The sooner they got on the road, the better.

But would they be able to leave?

The image of Nico's sorrowful face upon learning the crushing news that Pippo would not be permitted to make the trip to America flashed across Luca's mind. Perhaps he should have been more sensitive. More understanding.

More compassionate.

Perhaps he should not have been so hard on the boy nor dismissed his concern as though it were of lesser importance than everything else.

As Luca made his way down one of the hillside paths, his knees weakened at the thought that something terrible had happened to his son. How could Luca ever forgive himself?

And if Nico were still alive, how could the boy ever forgive him?

The trip to America now seemed meaningless in light of the current tragedy. But if Nico did not reappear soon, they would miss their train to Palermo and their ship to America.

Luca grit his teeth. There was no way he would allow Nico to keep them from their destiny. The boy simply must show up.

But what if he didn't?

Maria would never leave without Nico. Impossible.

There was only one thing to do: Find the boy.

And find him fast.

Dawn spread its wings over the countryside as Luca frantically searched the hillsides and fields of *Bella Terra*. Thankful that the light of burgeoning day now made his search easier, he trudged through grove after grove of orange and lemon trees. Row after row of peppers and eggplant and squash. His eyes scanned every single one as he called his son's name.

But no sight of Nico.

Where could the boy be?

Luca's stomach tensed as the sun burst over the horizon. No time to lose. If they did not leave within the hour, they would miss their connections. And Giulio, who was to meet them on Ellis Island, would be left wondering what had become of them.

The next ship would not leave Palermo for another three weeks, and there was no guarantee Luca could book passage for all of them on that ship. Manifests filled up quickly, especially since so many were leaving for the United States, not only from Sicily but also from all over Europe.

Worst of all, if he didn't report to his new job on October 1st, he would lose it.

His stomach churned as he hastened his steps back toward the house. A wild rabbit scurried in front of him, nearly tripping him as it fled into the underbrush.

Luca turned and, his hand shielding his eyes from the mounting sun, scanned the hills and fields one last time. When he was satisfied that Nico was not hiding in the countryside, Luca turned his face and his footsteps toward home, hoping that Salvatore or Maria had met with better success. There was nothing more he could do but leave the matter entirely in the Lord's hands. If God wanted them on that ship, God would have to get them on that ship.

But the question was: Did God want them on that ship? It was the same question he'd struggled with ever since making the decision to leave Sicily for America. Was Nico's disappearance a sign from God that they were not to go? An obstacle put before him to prevent the trip?

A warning of trouble ahead?

Once back home, he would have his answer.

Sweating from his frantic search, Luca climbed the hill toward the house, crossed the backyard onto the veranda, and entered the kitchen. To his great relief, Salvatore sat at the table with a sobbing Nico by his side. Pippo sat securely on Nico's lap, licking the boy's tear-stained face. Maria sat next to her child, her arm wrapped around his shoulders while her mother comforted Valeria and Anna who whimpered from all the turmoil.

Luca straightened and planted his legs wide. "Where were you?" His voice boomed in the large kitchen. "We've been crazy with worry!"

Immediately, he regretted his sudden outburst of anger. He should have at least greeted the boy and expressed his gratitude that he was alive and safe.

Luca's heart sank. "I'm sorry, son. I shouldn't have shouted at you that way."

Nico broke in. "Papa, I'm sorry for running away. I just can't bear leaving Pippo behind. I thought if I hid, I wouldn't have to go with you."

Heat flooded Luca's neck. "But did you think for one moment that we would leave without knowing where you were? Did you think we would leave you behind? Where was your head?"

Maria raised a palm in protest. "Luca, can't you see the boy is upset?"

"Not more upset than I am, I assure you. His actions have very likely caused us to miss our train and, possibly, our ship to America. Do you realize what that means?" He turned to Nico. "Son, what you did was wrong. And it could cost us our destiny."

Salvatore interrupted. "*Signor* Luca, everything is ready. The horses are swift. Perhaps we can make the train after all."

Luca released a weary breath. "Yes. We must leave now. I'm sorry about your dog, Nico. Pets are not permitted onboard the ship. The best I can do is get you a new dog in America."

Adamant in his stance, Nico sat with Pippo on his lap. "I'm not going to America."

Luca's blood boiled. "What do you mean you're not going to America?"

The boy lowered his eyes. "I mean I'm staying here with Pippo."

Luca raked his fingers through his hair. "Very well. Then we will leave without you."

Maria stood. "If Nico stays behind, I too will stay behind."

Luca's face burned. He stood to his full height. "I am the

head of this family, and I will decide what we do. Is that understood?" He pointed a finger at his son. "Nico, you are not yet an adult, and you are still under my parental authority. Therefore, you will do as I say. And I say you will come with us to America. Have I made myself clear?"

The clock struck the quarter hour past six o'clock.

Luca pointed an angry finger. "Now, I want all of you in that wagon within two minutes. And I want you to pray for a miracle that we make the train in time."

His heart pounded as he helped Maria and the children into the wagon. Maria's mother, sisters, and brother-in-law took their seats in the back of the wagon. The last to climb in was Nico. He'd spent the last remaining seconds bidding a heart-wrenching farewell to his beloved dog then handed him over to Felipe, another farmhand.

When everyone was seated, Luca took his place in front, to the right of Salvatore. He looked at the old farmhand and nodded. "It's time."

Salvatore cracked the whip on the back of the old white mare. "Bianca, you heard *Signor* Luca. It's time."

The old horse moved forward slowly and then, at Salvatore's prompting, broke into a full trot.

Luca drew in a deep breath. Would they reach the train station in time for their train's departure? Would they make it in time for the ship's departure?

Luca glanced back at Nico. The boy sobbed, his head resting on his chest.

Luca's throat tightened. Would his son ever forgive him for making him leave Pippo behind?

Chapter Six

Luca sat on the wooden aisle seat of the rickety, third-class train to Palermo. The train that allowed animals and produce to travel in the same cars with passengers. The train that stopped at every tiny village along the route to its destination.

Maria sat to his right in the middle seat, and little Valeria, in the seat by the window. Maria's mother, sisters, and brother-in-law sat in the seats behind them, with Anna shifting among their four laps.

Nico had found a seat by himself toward the front of the car.

His heart aching, Luca stared at the back of his son's head. Yes, they'd arrived at the train station in time, despite Nico's surprising, last-minute disappearance. Although still rattled by the ordeal, Luca was thankful they had not missed the train. But their departure had been riddled with badly strained feelings between him and Nico. Their good relationship of so many years was at risk of being damaged.

Perhaps damaged forever.

Luca's chest tightened as he turned to Maria. "Nico has wanted nothing to do with me since we left."

"Well, would you if you were he?"

His wife's words cut Luca to the quick. "It wasn't my intention to hurt the boy. Frankly, I'm feeling pretty sick about the whole thing myself."

"You could have handled it more compassionately." Her voice held reproach. "He's only a boy."

Another sting. Had he truly been heartless? Uncaring? Harsh?

"I guess you're right. It's just that his hiding from us at the last minute didn't help matters. It only added to the tension of the departure. We had so many other things to think about that looking for a lost son was not on my list of things to do." Did he detect a tinge of bitterness in his own voice?

Maria stiffened next to him.

His heart sank. Not only was his relationship with his son now strained, so was his relationship with his wife.

Things were not going as planned.

Rocking back and forth, the train chugged along the rusted track under a broiling late September sun, across the barren Sicilian countryside now arid with the effects of a second drought that had taken over the land and showed no signs of ending. Abandoned farms dotted the countryside. Lemon groves, once lush with lemons, now lay ruined with no one left to tend them. No wonder so many had left Sicily.

And continued to leave.

Not only had the economy collapsed, but the land no longer yielded an abundance of crops.

Only thorns and thistles.

And death and despair.

Luca wiped a hand across his forehead, lined with droplets of perspiration. The day had grown unbearably hot and humid, making it difficult to breathe. While the open windows allowed the entrance of a slight breeze, they also provided entry for gnats, flies, and mosquitoes. He swatted an annoying mosquito that buzzed around his ear, driving him to distraction. But, to Luca's dismay, the tiny creature escaped his deadly hand.

So much for being outwitted by a bug.

He glanced at the aisle beside him. The cackling of smelly, caged chickens close to his seat and the incessant buzzing of insects around his ears magnified the turmoil that rankled his heart.

And to think they had only begun their long journey.

Luca closed his eyes. Should he have allowed his son to bring Pippo, despite the sailing company's strict regulations against pets? Should Luca have written to the ship company for special permission?

Or chosen not to leave Sicily at all?

Had he inquired of the ship company, the powers-that-be might have made an exception for Nico.

Luca opened his eyes and let out a deep breath. Hindsight was always better than foresight. It was too late. The damage was done. All he could do now was make the best of a bad situation and hope and pray that Nico would get over the loss.

And that Maria would understand.

As soon as they were settled in Brooklyn, Luca would get Nico another puppy.

Although a new puppy could never replace Pippo, perhaps it would help the boy adjust more easily to his new homeland.

The matter was settled. Luca would make finding a new pet a top priority upon their arrival.

He placed a hand on Maria's. "As soon as we're settled in Brooklyn, I'll take Nico to buy a new puppy."

She turned toward him. "That would be a good idea. It will help to distract him from the memory and soothe his broken heart."

"And I think it would make you feel a lot better, too, wouldn't it?"

She smiled through weary eyes. "Yes, it would."

Luca put his arm around her shoulder and drew her toward him. Upon their arrival in America, he would ask Giulio to take him and Nico to the nearest dog breeder. Perhaps they'd even find another *Lagotto Romagnolo*.

Perhaps Nico would be happy once again.

Perhaps he and Nico would even be on good terms once again.

But what if having to leave Pippo behind had closed Nico's heart to Luca forever?

* * * *

A sweltering noonday sun beat down on Maria's head as she, Luca, and the children took the last, momentous step from dock to deck and boarded the *Argentina*.

Immigrants from all over Sicily, dragging trunks and carrying over-stuffed baskets of personal belongings, moved slowly forward in the long line that extended back to the pier.

The air smelled of squid and clams and seaweed. Fishermen in nearby fishing boats shouted at the top of their lungs while unloading the day's catch for distribution to local fish markets. Above the ship, seagulls soared and dipped in anticipation of a possible meal.

From the shore behind her, Maria's ears caught the sobs and sighs of heart-wrenching farewells, edged with the poignant pain of a permanence that was secretly feared but, nevertheless, outwardly denied.

Numb with grief, she placed one foot ahead of the other, following the long lines of boarding passengers like a sheep being led to slaughter.

Death must be easier than this.

Only a few moments before, she'd bid her final farewell to Mama, Luciana, Cristina, and Pietro. A farewell that had wrenched the very heart out of her for its foreboding finality. Very few immigrants who left Sicily got to see their loved ones again. Would she ever see Mama again? The dear lady was advanced in years and fragile. She'd barely survived the train trip to the port in Palermo. Would she survive a separation of several years? Who knew when they'd return to

Sicily again, if ever? They'd spent their life savings to get to this point. It would take several years of hard work to put aside enough money for a return trip.

Her shoulders shaking, Maria swallowed the sob that rose to her throat. The ship had not yet set sail. She could still turn back.

No. To do so would be cowardly. Unsupportive of her husband. Not to mention disobedient to God.

She must be strong. For her children. For herself.

For Luca.

Although he hadn't spoken much, she sensed his doubt about making the trip. So many obstacles had already threatened their purpose. What other obstacles lay ahead?

She drew Anna close to her heart while Luca followed close behind carrying Valeria. A forlorn Nico walked at her side, holding on to her elbow.

The poor boy. His heart, too, was broken. She glanced at him. "Are you all right, *figlio mio*?"

The tears in his dark eyes answered her.

"When we get to Brooklyn, we will get you a new puppy."

His clenched jaw was his only reply.

She prayed his heart had not hardened against Luca.

A ship official shouted ahead of them. "Keep moving forward. We have more than eighteen hundred people trying to crowd into steerage and not much time before departure. Please keep moving forward."

With Luca close behind her, Maria followed the crowds to the lower deck assigned to steerage passengers and made her way to an open spot at the railing large enough for her family to fit. Shielding her eyes from the brilliant sun, she stood at the railing holding Anna close to her heart. Overhead, dark clouds moved across the early afternoon sky while stiff gusts of wind warned of an impending storm.

The foghorn thundered, startling Maria, as it alerted passengers of imminent departure. Dozens of men, women, and children crowded the lowest of the three decks where Maria, Luca, and the children struggled to keep from being crushed.

Hot tears streamed down Maria's cheeks as her eyes strained to find Mama, Luciana, Cristina, and Pietro among the hundreds of friends and family members lined along the shore, waving a final farewell to their loved ones. Maria leaned against the worn railing, holding a squirming Anna close to her chest while Valeria tugged impatiently at her long black muslin skirt. "Mama, I can't see. Pick me up, too."

Before she could respond, Luca reached over and picked up their little one. "Come, my little treasure. You can sit on Papa's shoulders."

Valeria squealed in delight as Luca lifted her and planted her squarely across his broad shoulders. "Where's *Nonna*?"

Maria tensed. Where, indeed, was Mama?

At last spotting her family, Maria's whole body trembled as she waved a final farewell.

Maria lifted Anna's little hand toward Mama's small, fragile figure. "Wave bye-bye to *Nonna*." Maria's voice cracked. The poor woman leaned against Cristina, looking as though she would soon collapse from sorrow.

Maria's heart clenched.

Tears streamed down Mama's wrinkled face as she waved a crumpled handkerchief and stopped every few seconds to wipe the tears from her eyes.

Heart shattered, Maria waved in return, wondering if Mama could even see her among the multitudes lining the railing. It took every ounce of strength within Maria's soul to keep from jumping ship and swimming back to shore.

Luca stood at her side, holding Valeria, while Nico stood

to her right.

"I know how difficult this is for you." Luca placed his hand on her shoulder.

She bit her lower lip. Luca would never know how difficult it was. His parents were gone. He was leaving no one behind, other than some good friends. She was leaving Mama, her sisters, the home of her childhood.

Her very life.

The price Luca was paying could not compare to the price she was paying.

She swallowed hard, taking captive the negative thoughts that bombarded her. No. She would not allow resentment to poison her heart. She had left Sicily of her own free will. And she would endure the consequences of her choice.

No matter what those consequences would be.

She gazed at Mama standing on the shore, waving her tear-stained handkerchief. The image engraved itself on Maria's soul and would stay with her forever, indelibly imprinting her consciousness with overwhelming guilt. Her departure had brought this intense suffering upon her mother. Could Maria ever forgive herself? What if something happened to Mama because of Maria's decision to leave? What if Mama fell ill?

What if Mama died?

Maria pushed the horrible thoughts from her mind. She had enough to think about without worrying about matters beyond her control. She had done right to follow her husband.

Had she not?

Scripture said a man must leave his father and mother and cling to his wife. Did that verse apply to wives as well?

A loud wail from the shore pierced the early afternoon air, sending a chill through Maria's veins.

Maria turned toward Luca. "Luca, that was Mama! I would recognize her cry anywhere!"

Maria turned her gaze back toward the pier and, through stinging tears, searched for her mother. At the sight of Mama collapsing to the ground, Maria's heart lurched.

She gasped in horror. "Luca! Mama has collapsed!"

But there was nothing Maria could do. The ship had lifted anchor and was pulling away from the wharf.

Her heart constricted as she broke into sobs. Was Mama still alive?

The haunting question burned itself into Maria's soul, robbing her of all peace. It was a question that would not be answered for several grueling weeks. Only after she'd written a letter to her sister and received a response would Maria know the truth.

Could she endure for that long, not knowing if Mama were dead or alive?

As the ship left the dock, Maria's body left with it.

But her heart ripped away and remained behind.

* * * *

Luca drew Maria close to his heart in a vain attempt to comfort her. For a man who wanted to protect his wife from pain, there was nothing worse than the feeling of helplessness that flooded his soul upon watching her suffer. It would be weeks before they would hear about what happened to Mama. Whether she was still alive or had collapsed in death. Maria could not post a letter until they reached New York. Then it would take several weeks before the letter arrived at *Bella Terra*. Then Mama—or Cristina—would write back, and Maria would have to wait another several weeks before receiving their reply.

Luca swallowed the lump in his throat. Could Maria endure for so long the anguish of not knowing?

He glanced at his precious wife. Tears streamed down her cheeks as, sobbing, she waved a final farewell to a mother, two sisters, and brother-in-law now out of sight.

Luca's stomach clenched. Was he doing the right thing? Not only for himself, but also for his family? Had He heard God's voice? Or was he turning a new leaf in a book that would prove to be a worse story than the one he'd been living?

Regardless, it was too late now. They were on their way.

He stood at the ship's railing, his children at his side, Maria against his chest. The Sicily that Luca had grown to love was now nothing more than a speck against a gray sky.

Luca swallowed hard. For the first time since their departure, the prospect of leaving his beloved Sicily struck him with full force. He gazed one last time at the disappearing coastline. Could there be another place on earth as beautiful as this island? As woven into his soul as this country of his birth?

As close to his heart as this land of his ancestors?

What Sicily lacked in financial wealth it made up for in natural wealth. The breath-taking beauty of its shores and its mountains; the bounty of its oranges and lemons; the exquisite brilliance of its wildflowers and foliage—all would be indelibly etched in his mind and heart as long as he lived.

As would the magnificent people who had shaped his life.

His muscles tensed. Up to this point, leaving Sicily had been only a concept. An idea.

A plan.

Now it had become a reality.

A reality from which it was too late to turn back.

They were on the ship, leaving port. The crew had lifted anchor, and the ship was moving quickly toward the high seas.

With his sleeve, Luca wiped a tear from his eye. Anticipation mingled with anxiety as the ship pushed farther and farther out of Palermo Harbor toward the deep waters of the blue-green Mediterranean Sea. Rocking back and forth, the ship yielded itself to the waters. Overhead, gray clouds turned dark as an easterly wind beat against the hull.

A pewter-gray sky hung low above them, pregnant with a stifling humidity that made it difficult to breathe. Only a slight breeze from the Mediterranean Sea made the heat tolerable. The smell of salt filled the air and mingled with the aroma of ripened oranges and lemons packed away in the baskets of many of the passengers.

Luca's muscles tensed. Their departure had been bitter. Fraught with sorrow.

And, in the end, stabbed with fear.

Would their arrival be equally so? What lay ahead for him and his family? Had he really heard from God? If so, did obedience to God require the pain of seeing his wife suffer?

Tormenting questions bombarded his mind.

He lifted Maria's chin. "Are you all right?"

She turned toward him and, trembling, buried her face once again in his chest. A sob broke from the depths of her soul.

Little Valeria, perched on Luca's shoulders, placed her hand on Maria's head. "Mama, don't cry."

Maria lifted her face toward her little girl and smiled through hot tears. "Mama will be fine, darling. Don't worry."

Maria's reddened eyes broke Luca's heart. In their depths, he read the anguish of her soul.

He caressed her cheek. "It will be all right, dear one. Our heavenly Father is with your Mama. And He goes with us to the new land." Even as he spoke the words, he wondered. Did God go only with those who were in His will? What if he'd missed God's will? Would God still go with them?

Maria took his hand and held it close to her face. A tear rolled down her cheek. "I trust Him, Luca." She lifted her gaze toward him. "And I trust you."

Her words broke into the heaviness of his soul, bringing light. How thankful he was for the great gift God had given him in this precious woman!

Nico tugged on his sleeve. "Papa, pay attention. The crew-master has ordered passengers to find their berths in steerage. The line has started to move. We need to keep up."

Luca's concern for Maria had momentarily distracted him from the task at hand. "Thank you, son." At least, Nico had started speaking to him again.

The shrill sound of the foghorn's blast startled Luca as the *Argentina* plowed full-steam into the open seas of the Mediterranean. They were officially on their way. No more looking back. Only looking ahead. A gray sky, bent low with dark, heavy clouds, spread its ominous arms overhead.

Luca gathered his family from the lower deck railing and ushered them toward the stairwell that led to the steerage section. His stomach tightened into a knot. Steerage was the only class of travel he could afford for his large family. He'd heard of passengers contracting serious diseases as a result of traveling in steerage for days without fresh air or sunshine. Many had even died on board, before ever reaching their destination. He whispered a prayer for protection.

The ship turned and plowed ahead into the deep, dark waters of the Mediterranean Sea. The wind picked up while flashes of lightning streaked across the eastern sky, followed by large drops of rain.

Luca turned to his family. "We'd better go down to locate our quarters. This looks like a nasty storm. We don't want to be outside in it." Holding Valeria's hand, he led Maria, Anna, and Nico away from the railing toward the stairway into the steerage section. Crowds of passengers headed toward the same entrance, creating a bottleneck. "Nico, help your Mama with the basket."

"Yes, Papa." Nico took the basket from Maria's arm and placed it on his own. Then he pointed to the dark entrance into the ship's hold. "Papa, the stairs are over there."

Luca handed Valeria to Nico. "Son, you take care of Mama and your sisters while I drag this trunk down into the hold."

"What's 'the hold,' Papa?"

"It's the bottom-most area of the ship."

Nico's eyes widened. "Will we be under water?"

Luca forced a smile. "Yes, the steerage section is below the water line, but we will be inside, of course." Luca did not miss the concern in Maria's eyes.

The master-at-arms of the sailing company stood at the top of the stairway, shouting to the crowds. "Keep moving! Keep moving! We've got to get everyone settled fast."

A man to Luca's right raised a fist as he tried to keep his wife and baby from being crushed. "What do you think we are? Cattle?"

"Would that we were cattle!" another man rejoined. "Even cattle are treated better than this."

Luca stiffened. The angry exchange did not portend well for the trip. He kept Maria and the children close in his circle of protection.

The master-at-arms mumbled a curse under his breath then pointed an index finger in the direction of the stairwell. "The stairs are to the right. Descend two flights and you will reach the hold." He snarled through yellow teeth. "*Buon viaggio.*"

How could anyone have a good trip in these conditions?

Dragging the trunk behind him, Luca led the way down the long narrow flight of stairs to the steerage section. With each step, his heart sank lower and lower. Pungent odors of sweat, urine, and vomit rose from the hold, like foul fumes riding on putrid wings of disgust. Although the ships were cleaned between voyages, removing the odors of previous passengers holed away in tight quarters for several weeks was impossible.

Toilet facilities were minimal, and what facilities were available were filthy.

The farther Luca descended, the darker it grew. The sounds of crying babies mingled with the murmurs of complaining adults, all struggling to get comfortable in a place that defied all possibility of comfort.

"Papa, it stinks down here." Nico held his nose. "I can't breathe."

Luca's muscles tensed. "As soon as we're settled, we'll go back up on deck for some fresh air. We don't have to stay down here the whole time. Only when we sleep. We can spend our days on deck."

Luca's heart sank. They would be in the bowels of the ship for three long weeks. Not a happy prospect. Once again, he questioned his decision.

A rat scurried by and Valeria screeched. "Papa, I'm scared!"

Maria began to cough. "Luca, how are we going to tolerate this for three entire weeks? I'm worried about the children. This is a horrific dungeon."

Luca winced. Maria was right. It was, indeed, a horrific dungeon. What had he done by bringing his family here? Had he missed God? Had he followed his own prideful ambition?

But now was not the time to look back. Only one thing remained.

To go forward.

And to trust that God was leading them.

But would God lead them into this hell on earth?

Chapter Seven

It was after two o'clock in the morning when Will Dempsey collapsed into his bed. He'd had a rollicking night at O'Malley's Bar, downing several shots of whiskey and a good amount of rum before attempting to make his way home. Had it not been for the merciful help of Officer Casey McBride, Will would have spent the night in a gutter.

He lay in a stupor on his bed, his stomach aflame and his breath coming in half-gasps. Why did he never remember before he took the first drink what he'd have to suffer after he took the last?

A silver moon shone through the tenement house window, casting mournful shadows across the one-room flat he rented. Bleary-eyed and brain-boiled, he vacillated between sleep and wakefulness, cursing the night and longing for the dawn. Why, he didn't know. Dawn brought with it only a horrible hangover he'd spend all day Saturday fighting off.

If only Katie hadn't died.

When she was alive, he didn't drink at all. He'd witnessed firsthand what alcohol had done to his father.

He punched his fist into his pillow, fighting back the hot tears that stung his eyes. Life wasn't fair. God wasn't fair. Why did He have to take a woman who'd never harmed a soul and a kid who'd never hurt a fly? Why hadn't God taken a drunken bum like him?

Or an Italian?

Or a Jew?

Will's eyelids fell heavy over his eyes. He welcomed the numbness that cloaked his mind. It blocked the pain.

At least, for a little while.

Maybe he would do something to block it forever.

* * * *

With Valeria's little hand in hers and Nico at her heels, Maria clasped Anna close to her breast as they followed Luca to a far corner of the steerage section. Already, dozens of immigrants had arrived, dragging heavy trunks and carrying baskets of essential belongings—and some not so essential. All seemed just as dazed as Maria by the deplorable conditions surrounding them. Beleaguered mothers, with screaming toddlers in tow, followed weary young husbands in search of a resting berth for their families. Old women wearing multi-colored, patchwork headscarves, clinging to even older men wearing gray *coppola* hats, shuffled across the worn, splintered floor planks in search of a place to sit down and rest. Chattering adolescents, poking fun at one another, grew somber as they scanned the deplorable surroundings in which they would have to spend the next three weeks.

Rows and rows of bunks lined the walls, while numerous trunks and suitcases sat in the middle of the floor, many of them being used as temporary seats for weary travelers.

The smoke of a cigarette brushed against Maria's nostrils, smarting her eyes and inciting a cough. The stifling, stench-filled air was bad enough without adding cigarette smoke to the mix.

She turned to see where the smoke was coming from. A bronzed-skinned young man, wearing a slightly tilted *coppola* hat, cast leering eyes her way.

A chill ran through her. The nerve! He'd blown the smoke in her face to get her attention. She averted her eyes and tightened her hold on Anna. "Come, Nico. Let's hurry."

"I'm coming, Mama."

The dear boy had not once complained, despite his anguish at having left his beloved dog behind. Maria would get him a new dog as soon as they were settled in America. A new pup would never replace Pippo, but would, perhaps, distract Nico's attention from his pain.

Maria sighed. It was one thing for her to suffer. But to see her children suffer broke her maternal heart.

Weaving her way around the luggage, she kept her eyes fixed on Luca's back. It would be easy to get lost in the maze of people crowding into the tight quarters. The sounds of different Italian dialects caught her ears. Neapolitan. Sicilian. Calabrese. All were heading to America.

The hold was filling up quickly as streams of passengers made their way into the cramped quarters. How many would the ship allow in such a tight space? Already they were squeezed in like packed sardines. Would the ship be able to sustain the weight of so many people with so much cargo?

Valeria stumbled.

"Are you all right, darling?" Maria caught her just as an elderly passenger dropped his trunk ahead of them, nearly hitting the small child. Maria gasped.

"I'm tired, Mama. Please carry me."

Holding Anna in one arm, Maria stooped down to pick up her firstborn little girl with her other arm. Poor Valeria trembled from being shuffled in the frightening maze of adults dragging their belongings all around her.

Maria took a deep breath. With both of her daughters now in her arms, she continued to follow Luca.

Rows upon rows of unkempt bunks lined filthy walls that were interrupted only by a dirt-encrusted skylight here and there. In the empty space between the bunks stood long, spindly-legged tables used for eating meals, for conversation, and for playing games.

Not a single window broke the entire length of dirty

walls. A dull shaft of light fell from the staircase into the darkened quarters, soon dissipating into shadows the farther she and her family penetrated the dreary dungeon.

The foul odor of human excrement hung heavy in the air, sending wave after wave of nausea through Maria's stomach. She pressed her lips together to suppress the urge to vomit.

This was worse than the worst nightmare. A living hell on earth.

Nico drew up to her side. "Mama, it smells in here."

"I know, son. But there's nothing I can do about it now. As soon as we're settled, we'll go up on deck for some fresh air."

Her heart sank. How would her children survive this for three long weeks?

How would she?

Luca's voice interrupted her worrisome thoughts as he stopped at a set of bunks and matched the numbers on the tickets to the numbers on the bunks. "These are our bunks."

Maria stared in disbelief at what would be their living quarters for the next three weeks. Two bunks, covered with dingy straw mattresses, lay one atop the other, separated by slightly more than half a meter of space between them. Not enough room to sit up in bed without hitting one's head on the upper bunk or the ceiling. A single frayed blanket, stained with the sweat of previous passengers, lay shabbily folded at the foot of each bed. Torn pillows, looking more like tattered rags, lay at the head of each bunk.

Her heart constricted. She and Luca would take the lower bunk and the three children would squeeze into the upper bunk. The children would be safer there from any disturbance from unruly passengers.

Luca placed a gentle hand on her shoulder. "We'll take the lower bunk and place the children above us." He'd read her thoughts.

She nodded. An overwhelming longing for *Bella Terra* brought tears to her eyes. If only this were all a bad dream. If only she had decided to remain in Sicily.

If only, if only, if only ….

She must not dwell on the "if onlys." They were traps of Satan to rob her of her peace and to keep her from her destiny.

The incessant cries of small children pierced the air while harried mothers tried in vain to calm them. On the other side of the hold, a fight broke out between two young men over who would get the lower bunk.

Maria's heart sank. Not only were the surroundings deplorable, disgusting, and dangerous, but the horrible smells also made it nearly impossible to breathe. She coughed, her stomach roiling from the stench of urine and vomit that assailed her nostrils. As she covered her mouth in an attempt to suppress the nausea, a groan escaped her lips. How would she ever survive three weeks of this? And what of the children? The unsanitary conditions of the place would surely make them sick.

The very thought of illness made her insides shake. If she, Luca, or one of the children got sick, they might not be permitted to enter the United States when they arrived. Such had been the gist of the chatter around her as she'd waited in line to board. Frightening reports of the horrors awaiting them at Ellis Island floated among the passengers. Reports of children being deported without their parents. Of husbands or wives being turned away and forced to return to Italy without their spouses.

Of families being separated forever.

Maria cringed as shiver after shiver ran through her.

Only those passengers traveling in steerage were subjected to the grueling physical examinations at the Ellis Island port of entry. Physical and mental exams that did not consider the immigrant's exhaustion from a strenuous and taxing trans-Atlantic voyage. Exams that resulted in the branding of chalk letters on clothing when an illness was suspected—or even when only fatigue was the problem. Barbaric eye exams performed with dangerous metal buttonhooks.

The horrific reports among the passengers numbed her mind and made her tremble. What if she or Luca did not pass the exams? What if one of the children were not allowed entrance into the United States?

What if all hope of a better life were stolen from them?

She shut her eyes to block out the unbearable images assailing her mind. She wouldn't think that far ahead. She'd take only one day at a time. Had not the Lord said that each day's troubles were sufficient for that day?

Luca lowered the trunk to the floor at the head of the bunk then placed the large basket beside it. "You look exhausted, and the children are tired. Let's rest a while."

Her back aching, Maria lowered Anna and Valeria onto the lower bunk and dropped down next to them. Fatigue over-ruled all plans of covering the mattresses with the clean sheets she'd brought for the purpose. She would do that before they retired for the night.

Valeria squeezed her little four-year-old body between Maria and her baby sister. "Is this our new house, Mama?"

Maria drew her elder daughter to herself and forced a smile. "For just a little while. But soon we will be in a better place."

Soon could not come quickly enough.

Valeria wiggled out of Maria's embrace and crawled across the mattress. "I like this new house, Mama. It looks like a fort."

Maria winced at the sight of her daughter traversing the filthy bed.

Valeria giggled and motioned toward her little sister. "Let's play, Anna."

As in a flash of lightning, Anna joined her sister in crawling over the mattress. Despite the filthiness of the place, Maria did not stop them. To do so would be pointless since the entire area was infested with germs.

"Oh, look, Mama! A bug!"

Maria winced at the sight of dozens of tiny bedbugs crawling across the mattress. She turned to Luca. "Luca, we can't sleep here. The beds are infested with bedbugs."

Luca placed a hand on her shoulder. "I brought some eucalyptus oil for this very eventuality."

Relief flooded her soul as Luca removed the vial of eucalyptus oil from the large basket and sprinkled several drops across the upper and lower mattresses.

The bugs scurried into hiding.

"Look, Mama! The bugs are running away."

"Yes, Anna. And I hope they stay away."

As Maria watched, her two little girls began to romp and play. Oh, the innocence of children! They could turn the worst situation into a game of sheer delight. Perhaps she should follow their example.

She might not be able to change her surroundings, but she could at least change her attitude about her surroundings. Doing so would make the trip somewhat more bearable, if not completely so.

But changing her attitude would require the supernatural strength only God could give her.

And her willingness to accept it by faith.

The willingness was there. But was the faith?

* * * *

Luca lay wide-awake in his bunk as hurricane-force winds beat against the hull of the ship. The old vessel creaked and groaned, rocking wildly back and forth, desperately trying to hold its own against the headwinds that rammed into it.

Luca's stomach tightened. They'd been sailing for almost three weeks and would soon reach port.

If, that is, they survived this vicious storm.

He turned toward Maria.

Her wide-open eyes betrayed her fear.

"Are you all right?"

She shook her head. "Do you think we will survive?"

He stroked her cheek. "The Lord did not bring us this far, dear one, to abandon us."

Luca sat up on the edge of the bunk, his stomach roiling with nausea. Nearly every eye in steerage was awake, despite the lateness of the hour. Everywhere, people moaned or vomited upon their beds. The stench was unbearable, but this time, because of the powerful winds, they could not go up on deck for fresh air. The ferocious winds would hurl them overboard for sure.

Luca stood to check on the children. Thank God they were asleep, but probably not for long.

A steward walked by, handing out bread and apples. "These will help to calm the seasickness."

Luca took an apple and thanked him. "Is this storm unusual?"

The steward gave him a weak smile. "A bit stronger than most, but the old ship has seen worse."

The tone of the man's voice betrayed concern. "It should be over in a few hours."

Even another minute was much too long. Luca forced himself to bite into the apple. He needed to keep up his strength in order to take care of his family.

A sudden pitching of the ship knocked the fruit out of his hand and sent it rolling across the floor.

Screams broke out among the people as water began

pouring into the hold. "God, have mercy! We're going to die!"

Luca rushed toward the pouring water to see what was going on.

"Stay calm!" The steward's voice rose above the din. "It's just water flowing in from the deck. Some of the ceiling boards have fallen. Please. Do not worry!"

Together with the steward and several other men, Luca grabbed blankets, towels, and whatever they could find to plug the opening in the ceiling. But to no avail. The water kept pouring in, drenching him from head to foot. If they didn't do something fast, it would flood the entire steerage section.

Women screamed as the ship's violent pitching threw them and their children to the floor. Suitcases slid across the wooden planks, crashing into tables, chairs, and bunks.

Several people started running toward the stairwell.

The steward waved a hand and shouted. "Please, let me pass first. I must go on deck to get help."

But the panicked crowd persisted in its frantic attempt to escape the rising flood.

Luca ran back to Maria and the children. "We cannot stay down here. The hold is rapidly filling up with water. If we don't get out now, we may not be able to."

"Papa, I'm scared." Anna sat up on the upper bunk, rubbing her sleepy eyes.

"I am, too." Valeria reached for Luca.

He lifted her into his arms. "God will protect us, little one. There is nothing to fear."

He spoke the words as much for himself as for his daughter.

The ship climbed and plunged, climbed and plunged, at the same time rocking violently from side to side, pitching and heaving like a cobra poised to strike. With his free hand,

Luca grasped the wooden post supporting the upper bunk bed to keep his balance while he held his little one in his arms.

Maria stood beside him, her face white with fear. "Luca, let's pray. Jesus calmed a storm. He can calm this one, too."

Taking Maria's hand, Luca bowed his head. "Lord Jesus, You are here in our midst. As You did, and in Your mighty Name, we speak to this storm and command it to be still."

The ship continued to heave and dip, heave and dip, while angry waves crashed mercilessly against its hull.

All around them, passengers screamed and shouted obscenities at those who were holding up the line on the stairway.

Luca turned to Maria. "I think we should stay here. If we go up on deck, we could get blown overboard, not to mention knocked down by the crowd."

Maria nodded. "Yes. I think you are right. We prayed. God will answer us."

Within a few moments, the pitching began to diminish as the winds died down and the ship settled into a stable sailing pattern.

"Praise God!" Luca lifted his hands in thanksgiving.

"Thank You, Lord!" Maria's lips caught the tears of gratitude that streamed down her face.

Just then, the steward returned. "We have temporarily covered the damaged ceiling and will replace it with new boards at daybreak. But, have you noticed the storm has subsided?"

Luca smiled. "Yes. We prayed, and God answered our prayers."

The steward laughed. "I should take you on every voyage. You are a miracle-worker."

Luca grabbed the opportunity to witness. "I'm not the one you want to take with you. Accept Jesus as your Savior, and He will always go with you."

The steward feigned seriousness. "I will do that. First chance I get."

"Don't wait, my friend. You may not have another chance."

But by now the steward was gone.

Chapter Eight

Like a longed-for oasis in a dry, barren desert, New York City loomed large and welcoming in the hazy distance. Under the noonday sun that regaled a bright blue, late September sky, Luca stood at the worn railing of the crowded steerage deck, one arm around Maria's shoulder and his other arm holding Valeria. Nico stood to his side, holding two-year-old Anna.

A light gust of wind swept across the deck, spraying droplets of salt water over Luca's face. Droplets that mingled with the tears that ran down his cheeks. They'd arrived. They'd finally arrived in their new homeland.

But only by the grace of God.

The three-week ocean voyage had been nothing short of a nightmare. A nightmare that had seemed endless. But now it was over, and he could concentrate on building a future for Maria and the children.

As long as, that is, they passed the rigorous exams on Ellis Island.

His stomach twisted into a knot.

Those who had enough money to travel first or second-class had the luxury of being examined aboard ship before arrival and allowed to pass directly through customs and into New York. But those who had traveled in steerage had to pass through the long, grueling lines at Ellis Island before being admitted to the United States.

The ship rose slightly against the swell of the foamy, gray-blue waves. Moving north through the Narrows landing, it made its way through the choppy waters toward Upper

New York Bay and up the East River, slowly approaching the harbor.

Seemingly within arm's reach, the Brooklyn Bridge towered before Luca. He'd been told to look for it, in addition to the Statue of Liberty. The Bridge's solid structure conveyed a sense of permanence and stood as a monument to the immigrant who had designed it and to the immigrants who had built it, a testament to their determination, perseverance, and courage.

To the enduring hope that lay before them.

As the tip of Manhattan Island came into view, Nico shouted. "Papa, look! The Statue of Liberty!" The boy pointed excitedly at the stately statue just ahead. The world-renowned emblem of freedom that Luca had long admired in history books now rose high before him.

A symbol of the big, powerful country that was to be their home.

A reverential silence reigned on deck as the statue came into full view beside the vessel, all eyes riveted upon it.

His chest pounding, Luca lifted his gaze toward the world's great icon of freedom. His heart swelled at the sight of the imposing figure rising high before him. She towered, majestic and mighty above him, so close that Luca could almost touch her. How regal she looked!

His gaze searched her determined, uplifted face and circled the rim of her stately crown, proceeding upward toward the torch of freedom she held in her uplifted hand. She was far more striking that he'd imagined her to be. He could hardly keep his gaze off of her. Clad in her tarnished green garment, she raised her torch in warm welcome to those reaching the hallowed shores of the land of the free and the home of the brave.

Everything in Luca wanted to bow down and kiss her feet.

I am your God. There is no other.

The Lord's stern warning took him by surprise. Had he made America his idol before even setting foot on its soil?

God forbid!

He swallowed hard and whispered a prayer of repentance as the *Argentina* sailed past Lady Liberty toward the harbor. Just ahead, about a half-mile to the northwest, Ellis Island loomed large and menacing. It held the last major hurdle awaiting them before they would be allowed entrance into the United States.

The much-feared Ellis Island examinations.

Not only the physical exam, with its barbaric eye examination using the notorious button hook to check for trachoma, but also the long list of more than thirty questions to determine one's mental soundness and one's ability to support oneself once in the country.

Luca let out a long breath. Fortunately, he'd brought with him the amount of money required to enter his new country. Counting every coin he could find, he'd managed to save the twenty-five dollars required to assure the United States government he was well able to support himself and his family. Otherwise, they'd be turned away.

Within the span of the next few hours, their fate would be decided. Would they pass the physical, mental, and legal examinations? Would they be allowed entrance into America to begin their new lives? Or would they be temporarily detained or permanently deported?

A shiver ran through him. What if he or Maria didn't pass the exams? What if they would have to return to Sicily?

What if he did not fulfill God's call on his life to preach the Gospel in America?

During their trans-Atlantic voyage, he'd heard countless horror stories of the rigors awaiting them at Ellis Island, the point of entry dubbed the "Isle of Tears" and "Heartbreak

Island." The tragic stories bombarded his mind. Stories of families separated by the results of the examinations; stories of people being detained and hospitalized for weeks, some even to the point of death; and still of others being forced to return to wherever they'd come from.

That imposing fortress held within its pine walls the fate of all those who entered there.

The famous lines from Dante's *Inferno* flashed across Luca's mind:

Abandon all hope ye who enter here.

He resisted the negative thought. God was his hope, and he would trust in Him.

The foghorn boomed, startling Luca as the ship approached New York harbor for docking. Passengers began to stir. Some cheered. Some watched somberly.

Some quietly wept.

Luca turned to Maria. "We must prepare to disembark."

She nodded, her eyes revealing the anxiety in her heart.

Slowly, the ship pulled into the East River Pier and came to a halt. Crewmembers let down anchor then lowered the gangplank in preparation for the emerging crowds.

A light breeze brought some relief to the oppressive heat and humidity of late September in New York. Overhead, white clouds gave way to gray ones, portending a storm. Luca hoped they would reach shore before it broke.

He gathered his family to him. "Now, stay close together. It's easy to get lost in the crowd."

Cabin passengers disembarked first to the freedom awaiting them because of their status, while steerage passengers traversed the pier to a waiting area.

All around Luca, weary passengers slowly made their way toward the area where they would disembark. Exhausted mothers holding crying babies and holding tightly to cranky toddlers; anxious fathers dragging heavy trunks; nervous young women, dressed in long skirts and peasant blouses, carrying large bundles atop their heads; exuberant young men, eager to seek their fortunes; elderly married couples, leaning on their canes. And on each other.

Slowly Luca and his family made their way down the gangplank to the dock below. With the mastery of an experienced military leader, he guided his family off the ship and onto the wharf, leading the way as Maria and the children followed close behind. The strange sounds of the English language reached his ears. He'd tried to learn a few words on board ship, but he hadn't been too successful. He strained to hear his native tongue from one of the interpreters.

As they reached the dock, officials shouted directions followed by interpreters who interpreted the commands into several languages.

"All first- and second-class passengers go directly to customs. Steerage passengers, go to the barges to your right that will take you to Ellis Island." The official pointed in the direction of the barges.

Luca turned to Nico. "I will take care of carrying the trunk. You help Mama with the suitcases while she carries your sisters."

Luca took Maria by the arm. "This way, darling. We must board the barge that will take us to Ellis Island."

When they reached the waiting area for the barges, an official examined the name tags they had been given prior to disembarking. The name tags bore a manifest number written in large digits. "Numbers 31 to 60, this way, please."

Luca glanced at his family's name tags. His was 60, Maria's was 61, and the children bore 62, 63, and 64. He turned to the official and pointed to the numbers. "Please. Do not separate us."

The official frowned. "We are required to process you in

groups of thirty." He hesitated and then scanned Luca's family. "Very well—you may go with them."

Luca released the deep breath he had been holding. "Thank You, Father, for Your favor."

Already most of the barges had filled with passengers. Luca pointed to one that still had some empty seats. "Here, quickly. Let's grab some seats."

But before he could get his family aboard, others had rushed into the barge, claiming all of its places.

Luca let out a long breath. "We'll just have to wait for the next one."

Dragging the trunk behind him, he led his family to a nearby bench where they waited wearily for the next barge that would take them to Ellis Island.

After two long hours, an empty barge arrived. They would reach Ellis Island just before the cut-off time of three o'clock.

Luca handed over the family's belongings to a crew-member who piled them on the lower deck. Then Luca led his family to the barge's upper deck. Within a few moments, it was so tightly filled with immigrants that one could not turn around. The stench of perspiration and bad breath filled the air. Packed like sardines, they stood, unable to move. Whiny children tugged at their mothers' skirts. Luca kept a protective arm around his brood in a futile attempt to shield them from any more suffering.

The late afternoon sun burned brightly as the barge steersman untied the thick ropes and released the vessel into the waters. Luca gazed around him, taking everything in, trying to bring some semblance of order to his scattered mind. An eerie silence prevailed among the passengers, all of whom seemed just as bewildered, frightened, and confused as he. The next few hours would determine their fate.

He searched Maria's face. What was she thinking? Had

he been selfish in bringing her here? In putting her through so much suffering? "Are you all right, dear one?"

She smiled weakly and nodded. "I'm fine. It's the children I'm concerned about. They're cranky and tired. I can't wait till we are settled in our own home."

Their own home. According to what Giulio had written, their home would be a flat in a tenement house in Brooklyn. Giulio had made the arrangements and would meet them to take them there once their arrival had been processed at Ellis Island.

The barge reached the dock in front of the Great Hall where they would begin the examination process—a process that, from what Luca had learned aboard ship, could last as long as five hours. Luca gazed at the imposing building before him. Its pinewood façade seemed welcoming enough, although what lay behind its doors remained a complete mystery.

But not for long.

The barge slid into the slip along the pier and came to a total stop. A crewman lowered the gangplank and, one by one, passengers began to disembark. Gathering his family close to him, Luca led them off the barge and onto solid ground.

An official shouted orders. "Leave your belongings here!" He pointed in the direction of a building with a sign above it that read *Baggage Room.*

Luca followed the hundreds of men, women, and children who struggled with trunks, suitcases, and canvas sacks on their way to the Baggage Room. Placing the trunk in an empty space, he then took the bundles and basket from Nico and placed them beside the trunk where they would remain until after the examinations.

As they left the Baggage Room, an official handed out identity tags with numbers on them. "Men to the right!

Women and children to the left!"

Maria's eyes grew wide with fear. "Luca, they're separating us. What shall we do?'

"Don't worry. After the examinations, meet me right here at the Baggage Room. If I have not yet finished, stay here with the children until I return."

The officer shouted. "Keep the line moving, folks! We can't afford a backup!"

Luca didn't need an interpreter to understand the man's gestures and tone of voice. He whispered a prayer for protection for his family and their belongings. Then, waving toward Maria and the children, he followed the line of men toward the left and into the main building, all the while praying for favor and protection for himself and his family.

* * * *

Maria's heart sank as the Ellis Island official separated her and the children from Luca. She gave her husband a last, worried glance then proceeded to follow the line that was being shoved forward toward the large hall.

Uniformed guards greeted them and directed them to the examination areas where the processing would begin. Smells of body sweat, over-ripened fruit, and stale seawater hung heavily in the early evening air. Doctors, standing at intervals along the way, eyed each person for signs of poor health. Those who had trouble walking or breathing were pulled from the line for further examination. Farther on, other doctors instructed passengers to walk in circles to study them from all sides. Those with problems were marked with a large chalk letter on their clothing.

Maria held Anna tightly against her breast while Nico carried Valeria. "Stay close, Nico. If we do get separated, you know where to go afterward, right?"

"Yes, Mama. Where we left Papa—at the Baggage

Room."

She nodded. "Now, keep your wits about you."

He sidled up next to her and whispered. "Mama, what if I can't answer the questions?"

She saw the fear in his deep-set eyes. "Don't worry, son. Holy Spirit will tell you what to say."

The booming voice of an official speaking Italian interrupted Maria's thoughts. "This way, please. Stay in line. Keep moving forward toward the Inspection Room."

The Inspection Room. It sounded so ominous. So portentous.

So frightening.

She'd heard about it on the ship. It was the area where the dreaded three-part examination took place. Physical. Mental. Legal. Immigrants had to pass all three parts of the examination in order to be allowed admission into the United States.

A shiver ran through Maria's bones. *God, please help us!*

An official directed the people to the appropriate lines.

A second official held up a hand and stepped directly in front of Maria. "One moment, please. I need to check your names against the ship's manifest." Satisfied that all was in order, he then pointed to the examination area ahead and directed them to proceed.

The sounds of strange languages caught Maria's ears. She'd stepped into another world, a world that filled her heart with anticipation, but at the same time made it tremble.

Some immigrants, stopped by physicians on the stairway, already bore white chalk letters on their clothing, indicating their physical or mental condition. Thanks to conversations she'd overheard aboard ship, Maria knew that an "L" meant lame, "H" meant heart problems, and the letter "X" in a circle signified mental illness.

What would happen to these unfortunate ones? Would they be detained? Hospitalized?

Deported?

Her muscles tensed at the sight of a white-haired doctor a short distance ahead using the dreaded buttonhook to examine people's eyes. While on the ship, she'd overheard an elderly man describe this frightening instrument used to lift the eyelid in order to look for any trace of trachoma, a highly contagious eye disease that would warrant immediate deportation back to one's country of origin.

Nico leaned into her and whispered. "Mama, the button-hook doctors! Do you remember the old man from Palermo talked about them on the ship?"

Maria nodded, her jaw squared and stiff, but said nothing.

With each step forward, her heart raced more and more. The line moved steadily toward the highly feared doctors performing the eye exams. Soon it would be their turn to have their eyelids turned upward by the horrid buttonhook. Maria couldn't decide which was worse: To have the buttonhook used on her eyes or to be deported back to Sicily.

Suddenly, a woman in front of her let out a blood-curdling wail. "No, I can't go back! I must see my husband! We've been separated for seven years!" She began to sob uncontrollably. "Please. Please, have mercy."

Maria watched in horror as two officials gently led the poor woman away. Then Maria's heart stopped.

She was next in line.

* * * *

Will glared at Tony Sinclair.

The workshop delivery boy stood before him, trembling under the man's wrath.

"If you breathe a word of this to Cramdon, I'll kill you!" Will shook Tony by the shoulders. "Do you hear me, boy?"

Tony nodded, flinching at the venom pouring from Will's foul mouth.

Will sneered. The kid had gotten his point.

The night before, on his way home from the Italian Social Club, Tony had discovered Will sprawled on the third-floor fire escape, drunk as a tree shrew. Fearing Will would fall to his death, Tony picked him up, dragged him inside, and, lacking the key to Will's apartment, left him asleep in the hallway, just outside the door. When Will awoke the next morning, he had a faint recollection of the whole incident.

Embarrassed to question the boy, but even more curious to know exactly what happened, Will had called Tony into his office. Will wanted to be sure the kid wouldn't snitch on him to Oliver Cramdon, his boss. There were a few things Cramdon would not tolerate, and one of them was alcohol. If he found out Will was a drunk, Cramdon would fire him on the spot.

Will released the boy. "Glad we understand each other." Will pointed a crooked index finger in the boy's face. "Remember one thing: If I lose my job, then you lose yours. Understood?" Technically, the only way the boy could lose his job was if Will fired him before Cramdon fired Will. But Tony didn't need to know that. He just needed to be scared enough to keep his mouth shut.

Will motioned toward the door. "Now, get out of here! And from now on, mind your own business."

"Yes, Mr. Dempsey." Cap in hand, Tony turned and flew out the door like a scared cat.

Will took a deep breath and collapsed into his rickety, old swivel chair. A wave of guilt washed over him. He'd been too hard on the boy. Tony had only been trying to help. But Will had been worried more about himself than the boy's feelings.

Will pushed back the ache in his throat. What had happened to him? He'd turned into a mess of a man. A hard-hearted, self-centered coward who hated everyone including himself. Good thing Katie hadn't lived to see him like this.

But maybe if she'd lived, he wouldn't be like this.

He swiveled toward the tall window and stared at the Brooklyn Bridge, towering nearby above the building. Framed by a blue-gray, late September sky, it exuded a strength he was fast losing.

Over the past thirteen years since the bridge's construction, Will had greeted it every morning when he arrived at his office. How excited he'd been when he'd taken Katie and Willie for their first buggy ride across the bridge! From its height, they could see the tenement house where they lived and where Will worked. Six-year-old Willie had shouted, "Look, Daddy! I can see your office from here."

Willie had reached for his father's hand and pointed it toward the building. "See. Right there!"

Will swallowed hard. What would Katie and the kid think of him if they saw him now?

He pushed aside the painful thought and turned back to face his desk. This alcohol problem had gotten the best of him. At first, it had been only an occasional drink here and there. But after Katie and the kid died, he started drinking every night to drown out the pain. Before he knew it, he'd become dependent on the stuff, so dependent that he couldn't survive a day without it.

But he had no place to turn. No one who could help him. No one with whom he could share his problem.

Truth be told, he was too proud for that.

And too self-sufficient.

He raked his fingers through his hair. He'd handle the problem on his own. The way he'd handled every other problem on his own.

A chill ran through him. But could he trust Tony?

If word leaked out that Will Dempsey was an alcoholic, then he'd lose not only his job, but also any chance at another job. No one deliberately hired alcoholics. They were too risky. Employers couldn't count on them to show up, to produce, to stay on the job. No. An alcoholic was nothing more than a huge liability to any business.

The old despair settled in Will's soul. Maybe he should end it all. What did he have to live for anyway? A future that held no hope of anything better than he'd already had. What could be better than Katie and the kid?

A tear trickled down his cheek. He brushed it away. Big boys didn't cry. Cramdon wanted work on the Christmas orders to start early this year. Predictions were for big sales, bigger than any year in the past.

And Will was the one responsible to see that workers were hired and work was produced.

He opened the upper-right hand drawer of his desk and removed a cigar from the cigar box. That Luca guy should be arriving from Italy soon. Giulio said he was good. Real good. Will would put him on overtime as soon as he got here. And milk him for whatever he was worth.

Will leaned back in his chair and smiled. Milking Italians gave him a wicked pleasure unlike any other.

Chapter Nine

Five hours and several terrorizing moments later, as a new moon rose in the indigo sky, Luca led Maria and the children off the ferry and on to the dock where Giulio waited to greet them.

"Luca! Luca Tonetta!" A smiling Giulio hurried toward Luca, arms outstretched. "Welcome to America!"

Luca embraced his old friend and former customer then turned toward Maria. "Maria, this is my friend Giulio Genova."

Maria extended her hand in greeting and smiled. "Pleased to meet you, *Signor* Genova."

Giulio took her extended hand. "The pleasure is all mine, *Signora*." Giulio winked at Luca. "I see you've done very well for yourself, my friend. A beautiful wife. Three beautiful *bambini*. You are a wealthy man, indeed."

"Thank you, Giulio."

"And now, I know you are exhausted from the long voyage, so I will take you directly to your flat where you can rest and have something to eat after your harrowing day."

"Harrowing, indeed!" Wrapping an arm around Maria, Luca and his family followed Giulio toward a horse-drawn buggy that waited at the entrance to the port. As they rode toward Brooklyn, Luca caught up on his friend's life in America while sharing a bit of their experiences traversing the high seas.

After an hour, they reached the tenement house where Giulio had rented a flat for them.

"Here we are!" Giulio shouted. "Home, sweet home!"

Luca's heart sank. What could be sweet about the rundown building standing before them? Its cracked, concrete façade, covered with soot and graffiti, rose to six stories of individual apartments, each housing an immigrant family. Rusted fire escapes snaked up and down along its side, laden with drying laundry, broken clay pots, and, despite the lateness of the hour, dirty, rag-clad little children. Here and there, a shattered windowpane rattled against the evening breeze that carried the sounds of crying babies, shouting mothers, and demanding husbands.

On the fourth-floor level, a huge sign attached to the building read *Oliver Cramdon, Clothing Manufacturer.*

The driver brought the buggy to a halt and Giulio descended first. Luca followed close behind and then helped Maria and the children to descend.

"This is the Bensonhurst neighborhood." Giulio took Luca by the arm. "Mostly Italians live here, with a few Jews in the mix." He pointed to the building. "Your flat is on the third floor, across the hall from mine. Our workshop is on the fourth floor."

For a moment, Luca stood, heart sinking, in front of the dilapidated building in which they would live. Images of beautiful *Bella Terra* flashed across his mind, making the sharp contrast even more painful. What had he done bringing his family here? Had he brought them from the frying pan into the fire?

And what was Maria thinking?

He glanced over at her. Her dark eyes spoke volumes, but she said not a word.

Luca swallowed the ache at the back of his throat. Too late now. They would simply have to make the best of things until he could afford to get them out of here and into a decent house. "Very well. Let's get the luggage unloaded and carry it up to our flat."

Giulio, the driver, and Luca unloaded the wagon.

Giulio intervened. "Follow me. We need to go up to the third floor."

Luca turned to Maria. "You and the children go first. We will be right behind you with our belongings."

Satisfied that Maria and the children were safe in front of him, Luca dragged the trunk up the three flights of stairs while Giulio and the driver carried the two bundles. Nico carried the food basket.

Once on the third floor, they made their way through the narrow hallway, reeking of fried garlic and olive oil, to flat number three hundred thirteen, the place they would call home.

Giulio caught his breath. "This is it. Number three hundred thirteen." He gave Luca a broad smile and handed him the key.

"Thank you, my friend."

"Don't even mention it. It's the least I can do for the best tailor in the world."

Luca unlocked the door and the three men carried in the trunk, the bundles, and the basket.

His face perspiring, Giulio turned to Luca. "Once you are settled, I will make good on my promise to prepare for you the best Italian meal this side of the Atlantic."

Luca smiled. "I look forward to it."

After bidding farewell to Maria and the children, Giulio turned to go but then turned back again. "I almost forgot. Mr. Dempsey has scheduled you to begin work on the first of October. Only a week away. Our workshop is in this very building, on the fourth floor, so you will not have to travel far." He waved a dismissive hand. "But, of course, I will see you before then. If you have any questions or needs, just knock on my door. Goodnight, my friend. And, once again, welcome to America!"

Wiping his sweaty brow with a red-checkered handkerchief, Giulio smiled and left.

Luca looked around the tiny, one-room flat. A single door looked out over a small balcony. There were no other windows except the ones on the door. A tiny bathroom held a toilet and a small sink. On one wall stood an old iron stove, left uncleaned by the previous tenants, and, next to it, a filthy kitchen sink. On the other wall was a bunk bed consisting of two bunks, the top of which nearly reached the ceiling.

The ship's hold looked better than this.

Luca's gaze flew to Maria. His heart lurched.

She was weeping.

* * * *

Hot tears streaming down her cheeks, Maria stood trembling in the center of her new home. The knot in her stomach grew tighter the more she looked around. The dingy walls, the splintered wooden floors, the cobwebs encircling the single dim light bulb hanging from the ceiling—all combined to drive her heart to her feet. Not to mention the acrid smells of leftover dinners filtering in through the cracked, soot-covered door panes, and the shouts of neighbors fighting through paper-thin walls.

She'd left *Bella Terra* for this? Even the worst poverty in Sicily was no match for what surrounded her. At least at *Bella Terra* she'd had the open fields filled with acres of wildflowers, the wide expanse of indigo sky studded with millions of brilliant stars, the chorus sounds of chirping cicadas singing in the middle of the night. Here, instead, she had concrete walls, trash-littered streets, and tall rooftops that all but hid the sky. Here angry shouts from quarreling neighbors replaced the calm serenity of the night-time sounds of *Bella Terra*.

She'd gone from heaven to hell.

And there was no way out.

She forced back a sob. How would they manage in a one-room flat with only a narrow balcony for a playground for the children? With no backyard to hang the clean laundry?

With no privacy for her and Luca?

How could she spend her days cooped up in this hole where cockroaches scurried back and forth in the corners and mosquitoes arrogantly assumed squatters' rights?

This was a nightmare worse than the one on board the ship. At least that nightmare was only temporary. This one was permanent.

She covered her face with both hands. *Oh, God. Give me Your strength.*

Luca's arm surrounded her shoulders.

She burst into tears and buried her face in his broad chest.

He gently stroked her hair. "It will be all right, darling. Do not be discouraged. Once I earn enough money, I'll get us out of here and buy you a new house of your own. You can choose exactly the one you want."

From the tone of his voice, he, too, was heart-broken at their living arrangements.

With the back of her hand, Maria wiped the tears from her eyes. The hour was late, and the children were hungry. She would prepare a bite to eat before settling them in for the night.

An old table with four rickety chairs stood next to the bunk beds. Maria opened the large basket and took out some dried fruit, nuts, and a stale loaf of bread she'd taken from their daily portion during their ocean voyage. She set the food on the table.

Luca stood at the head of the table while Maria and the children filled the three chairs. They would have to buy another chair soon.

Luca took her hand. "Father, we thank You for the food we are about to eat. We thank You for bringing us safely to this land and to this place. We dedicate our new home to You, Lord. Bless it and fill it with joy and peace. Amen."

Joy and peace? That would take a miracle.

Maria took some chipped plates from the cupboard and placed some of the dried fruit and bread on them for the children. "*Mangiate.* You need your strength after our long trip."

"Mama, look at all the lights outside." Valeria pointed to the apartments across the courtyard. Through the open windows, one could see directly into the neighbors' living quarters. Maria cringed. She must remember to make a thick curtain for the window.

Nico reached for another slice of bread. "Mama, there were boys playing outside when we arrived. Maybe they could be my friends."

Maria's muscles tensed. "Boys shouldn't be playing outside this time of night. They should be home in bed."

"But I'm not in bed, Mama."

"You have good reason to be awake. We just arrived after a long trip. But now that we are here, you will not linger outside after dark."

Nico frowned. "Yes, Mama."

Luca touched her arm. "Maria, don't be too hard on the boy. He does need friends, you know."

Heat rushed to her cheeks. "I'm not being too hard on him, Luca. I don't know what kind of children live here. For all I know, they could be *scugnizzi*, rebellious ragamuffins always getting into trouble."

"For all you know, they could be very good boys."

She bit her tongue. There wasn't even enough room to have a private conversation in this place. At least at *Bella*

Terra, she and Luca could retreat to another room in private. But here, they'd have to confine every discussion to the time after all the children were asleep. And even then, she couldn't be sure their conversation would not be heard either by the children or the neighbors through the paper-thin walls.

She tore off a piece of bread and bit into it. It was stale. As stale as her life had become. Would she ever taste of fresh bread again?

I am the Bread of Life.

The Lord's words convicted her. She needed them. Needed the reminder that He was still with her and always would be. *Yes, Lord. I will choose to feed on Your blessings and not on discontent.*

"Is this our new house, Mama?" Anna's question pierced Maria's heart.

"Yes, darling."

"I like it, Mama."

Her daughter's words took Maria by surprise. "You do?"

"Yes, Mama."

"Why do you like it?"

"Because we are all together in one room."

An arrow pierced Maria's heart. *Out of the mouths of babes.*

Togetherness. Wasn't that what family was really all about?

For the first time since she left Sicily, a ray of hope touched her soul. She smiled in spite of herself. "Yes, Anna. What matters is that we are all together. That is what makes a home."

Anna's broad grin brought joy to Maria's soul. The miracle of joy Luca had prayed for.

And with the joy came peace.

* * * *

On his first day of work, Luca rose before dawn. Although his workshop was on the floor above, he wanted to allow himself time to pray before beginning his day. It was a habit he'd practiced ever since becoming a Christian years earlier.

A habit that had served him well.

He rose quietly so as not to disturb Maria. Sliding his feet into his slippers, he shuffled toward the stove to prepare a pot of espresso coffee. The children were sound asleep. Through the glass-paned door leading to the balcony, night gradually melted into the first gray-blue shades of a new day. Soon the sun would rise, although he would not be able to see its rising because of the tall tenement houses that surrounded him on every side.

His mind drifted back to the purple mountains of Pisano, and a lump formed in his throat.

Forget those things that are behind and press on toward the mark of the prize of your high calling in Christ.

The Lord's reminder brought him back to his senses. Better to forget the past and focus on the future. God had brought them here, and God would take care of them.

The coffee pot began to sputter. Luca removed the pot from the heat and poured himself a cup of the dark, steaming brew. There was nothing like a cup of espresso to start off the day. Outside, the sounds of a new day floated upward from the street below. Vendors plying their wares. Grocers setting up their vegetable stalls on the sidewalks.

Fish vendors bringing in the morning's catch.

In a way, the scene reminded him of Pisano.

But why not? These were Italians. His own people who had established a new little Italy in this Bensonhurst section of Brooklyn.

They'd been in their new flat barely a week, but already it was starting to feel like home. Over the past week since they'd moved in, they'd met several of their countrymen. Many lived on the same floor. They'd also met a lot of Jewish immigrants. The Jews and the Italians had a lot in common. Although their cultures were different, their outgoing temperaments were similar in many ways.

He gazed at Maria, still asleep on the makeshift bed they'd set up next to the bunk beds. The arrangement allowed Nico the upper bunk for himself, while Valeria and Anna shared the lower one.

Luca took a sip of the hot espresso. His stomach churned at the prospect of beginning his new job, at the thought of working for someone else. As a child, he'd worked with his father and then taken over the family business. Working for an employer was foreign to him. Especially an American employer. Italians understood other Italians, but Americans who'd been in the country for a few generations seemed like a different breed.

Besides, Giulio had mentioned in passing that Will Dempsey was a demanding boss who pulled no punches.

Luca carried his cup of espresso to the chair by the window and sat down. Taking his Bible from the window ledge, he opened it and began to read. His eyes fell on Proverbs 16: 3: "Commit your work to the LORD, and your plans will be established." Luca prayed. "Father, I commit this job to You. Establish my thoughts as I serve my employer. Let Your favor rest upon me. Help me to be a witness of Your love to all who cross my path. I pray in Jesus' Name. Amen."

Maria's rising interrupted him.

He turned toward her. "Good morning, Sweetheart. May I get you some coffee?"

She stretched, yawned, and then rose from the bed. "Yes, thank you."

He rose to pour her some coffee.

She took the *demi-tasse* cup from him and thanked him.

"How do you feel on this first day of your new job?"

"A bit nervous, to be honest. I've never worked for anyone else before." Luca let out a deep breath. "One day, I hope to have my own business again."

"That would take a lot of money."

His heart sank. "Yes, it would, but I'm still going to try. Perhaps I could set up a shop right here in this Italian neighborhood."

"Wouldn't that put you in competition with your employer?" Maria took a sip of coffee.

"I hadn't thought of that. And I would be no match for a large manufacturer like Oliver Cramdon." He gazed at her beautiful dark eyes, eyes that had recaptured their light. 'Maybe we could move to a better neighborhood where I would be the only tailor."

Hope filled her smile. "That would be a wonderful goal. Then we could get out of this straight-jacket of a place and have room to stretch."

He did not miss the longing in her voice. "Are you really that unhappy here?"

"Well, I can't honestly say I love it. Compared to *Bella Terra*, this is a slum."

He couldn't deny the truth of what she said.

She sighed. "But I am doing my best to be content in whatever state I am."

"At least we are not in a real prison, like the Apostle Paul." He put his arms around her. "Maria, I promise I'll make it up to you. I promise you with every breath in me that one day I will get you out of this wretched place. I hope that day comes soon. Meanwhile, let's make the best of it and be grateful for what we have."

She nodded. "That's all we can do at this point. I promise you I will make the best of it. For your sake and for the children's."

He kissed her lips. "Thank you."

118

She returned his kiss.

"Well, I'd better get dressed and get to work."

"I'll prepare some bread and cheese for your breakfast. I've packed you a lunch with some fruit in case you get hungry throughout the day."

He kissed her on the forehead. "Thank you, my love."

Having eaten and dressed, Luca bid Maria and the children goodbye and headed for the stairway that led to the clothing workshop. A large sign that read "Oliver Cramdon Clothing Manufacturer" greeted him just above the door that opened onto the fourth floor.

Luca walked through the door and into a long hallway with several rooms on either side. Each had a sign above it designating its purpose. He looked for the room whose sign read "Office." He and Giulio had arranged to meet there so that Giulio could introduce Luca to his new boss, Will Dempsey.

Heart pounding, Luca opened the door and entered the small room. No one was there yet. He'd arrived early so as not to miss Giulio.

Through the window, towering before him, stood the magnificent silhouette of the Brooklyn Bridge. The sight took Luca's breath away. Everything in America was so big.

He stood by the door, uneasy and unsure what to do. Perhaps he should wait outside.

Just as he turned to exit the room, a tall man pushed through the door. He stopped suddenly, narrowing his dark eyes. "Who are you and what do you want?" The man's voice was harsh.

Although Luca floundered to understand his words, the meaning of the man's gestures was unmistakable. "Luca Tonetta." He handed the man the work papers Giulio had obtained for him.

Will tore the papers from Luca's hand and read them. "So, you're the new Italian I hired." He looked up. "I'm your new boss. Will Dempsey." Will pointed to a chair. "Sit down."

Luca's muscles tensed. They were not off to a very good start. Where was Giulio?

At that moment, Giulio entered the office.

Luca breathed a sigh of relief.

"I'm sorry I'm late." Giulio spoke to Luca in Italian.

"What did you say?" Will's voice was gruff. "There will be no secrets in Italian—do you hear me?"

Giulio winced. "I'm sorry, Mr. Dempsey. But Mr. Tonetta does not speak English."

"He doesn't, does he?" Will gave a sardonic laugh. "Well, he'd better learn, and learn right away. How can he take orders if he doesn't speak English?"

"May I interpret for him, Mr. Dempsey?"

"What choice do I have if I want him to understand me? And while you're at it, tell him he'd better take English lessons, or else?"

Luca tensed at the way Giulio cowered before Will. "Or else what, Mr. Dempsey."

"Or else he's fired!"

"Yes, Mr. Dempsey. I will tell him." Giulio proceeded to interpret for Luca.

Luca's face grew cold as the blood drained from it. Where would he get the money for English lessons? He'd hoped to learn the language in the normal course of daily life. He hadn't considered that his lack of knowledge would interfere with his job. He turned toward Giulio. "Please tell Mr. Dempsey I will do whatever I need to do to keep my job."

Luca studied Will's face as Giulio interpreted Luca's response into English. This was not going to be an easy relationship.

Luca's stomach tightened. What if Mr. Dempsey decided there would be no relationship at all?

Chapter Ten

Luca followed Will and Giulio into the large workshop. Except for Will's personal office, the workshop occupied the entire fourth floor of the tenement house. There was one main room where workers did the cutting, the basting, and the sewing, each in a different section of the room. To the right of the main room was a supply room where the fabric was stored. On the opposite end was the pressing room where finished garments were pressed and hung for delivery to area department stores.

The room buzzed with the rhythmic whir of sewing machines, the loud rumble of rolling carts transporting large skeins of fabric across the worn wooden floors, and the light banter of friendly chatter and daily shop talk. Dirty light bulbs, attached to long, rusted chains, hung from the high ceilings over every workstation. Along the walls, open casement windows let in the brisk October air laden with the smell of diesel fuel from the nearby elevated train that stopped every half hour to deposit its passengers en route to and from Manhattan. The diesel smell mingled with the pungent fumes of the kerosene stove that sat in the far corner.

Luca coughed. Would he ever grow accustomed to city air?

From four floors below rose the shouts of vendors plying their wares amid the shouts of unruly little children playing in the streets.

Luca drew in a deep breath to help loosen the tight knot in his stomach. This was a far cry from his shop in Pisano. How would he fare here? Would he fare as well?

Would he fare at all?

Doubt niggled Luca's soul. A doubt riddled with a sense of dread that he would one day regret taking this job.

Luca stopped short as Will halted at a long table where three workers sat in wooden chairs and skillfully operated their sewing machines. The fourth chair was empty.

Will pointed to the empty chair and then turned to Luca. "This is your workstation."

All eyes turned toward Luca. One was a kind eye. One was a twinkling eye.

One was a seductive eye.

Luca tensed at the sight of a woman at his workstation. Here he would not be able to observe his old personal rule of not working with any woman other than his wife. But here, at least, he was not alone.

Will's voice interrupted his thoughts. "You will report for duty here at exactly 7:00 am every morning, on time, and you will work here until exactly 7:00 pm every evening. You will sign in upon arriving and sign out upon departing. A bell will go off to alert you to the time. You will be allowed thirty minutes for lunch and two ten-minute breaks, one in the morning and one in the afternoon. No violations of the rules will be permitted. If there is a violation, you will be punished severely, even, if necessary, to the point of losing your job. Each day you will have a quota of garments to sew, based on the demand. You will fulfill that quota each and every day. If you have not completed your quota by 7:00 pm, you will remain after hours until you complete it, no matter how long it takes. Is that understood?"

The man did not mince his words. Luca nodded as Giulio interpreted. Luca didn't need to know the words in order to understand that Will Dempsey meant business.

Will continued. "This workshop is owned by Oliver Cramdon. He is a demanding man and will not tolerate laxity or laziness of any kind on the job. He visits periodically to ensure that we are meeting his standards." Luca tensed at Will's gaze squarely upon him. "If Cramdon is not happy, then I'm not happy. Understood? My job depends on how well you do yours. So you'd better do it well."

At Giulio's translation, a shudder coursed through Luca's veins. Will Dempsey was not a man to be crossed in any way.

Nor was Oliver Cramdon.

"You will be working with Jake Goldberg." Will pointed to Jake who offered Luca a warm and welcoming smile.

Luca extended a hand toward Jake and smiled in return. At least one person was friendly around here. He was going to like Jake.

Across from Jake sat Gennaro Cappadona. "*Benvenuto.*" Gennaro smiled. "Welcome."

Another friendly face. "*Grazie!*" Luca shook his hand as well. How good to meet a fellow Italian with whom he could converse! At least something was going right for him today.

Will continued with the introductions. "And this is Paulina Ivanov."

Will's voice softened, and Luca's spirit went on high alert.

Paulina eyed Luca up and down and then gave him a provocative smile.

Luca braced himself. Not only did he have his work cut out for him in this place; he also had his spiritual warfare cut out for him. *Lord, give me wisdom.*

Will turned to Giulio. "Now, I've got work to do. I'll leave it to you to explain the ropes to your friend in your native tongue. Show him around. And tell him in no uncertain terms that I expect results. No results, no job! Is that clear?"

Hands on his hips, Will gave Luca a stern, warning look

and then left.

Giulio proceeded to interpret for Luca all that Will had said. "If you have any questions, my friend, please ask me." Giulio patted Luca on the shoulder. "And don't worry. Mr. Dempsey is more bark than bite."

Despite Giulio's attempt to encourage him, Luca had his misgivings. His first encounter with Will did not bode well for their future work relationship. Had Luca made a mistake taking this job? "Thank you, Giulio. I hope you're right."

"Trust me, Luca. I'm right."

But there was nothing Luca could do except move forward trusting God.

After Giulio left, Luca took his place at his workstation. Directly across from him, Paulina Ivanov smiled and batted her long eyelashes. "So glad to have you join us." She spoke with a Russian accent.

"Thank you." Luca gave her a tentative smile in return. "One day I would like you to meet my beautiful wife and three wonderful children."

Her smile turned to a frown. Without another word, she returned to her work.

Better to set the record straight from the start. Luca had enough to think about without worrying about a flirtatious woman on the job. Besides, the enemy would do anything to thwart his calling to preach the Gospel.

As long as Luca remained vigilant, the enemy could not defeat him.

* * * *

Will hurried back to his office. His introduction to Luca Tonetta had been far from what he'd expected. Will's gut feeling upon meeting him had been intense dislike. Hatred almost.

Nor did the fact that Luca was Italian help matters. As

much as Will tried to be unbiased, he couldn't help but feel that Italians were inferior to other people. Their general lack of schooling, their slovenly ways, and their isolationist habit of keeping among themselves did little, if anything, to promote their social and economic advancement. Despite their protests to the contrary, Italians seemed intent on eating their pasta, laughing at life, and getting by with as little effort as possible.

His stomach hardening, Will settled into his old swivel chair.

Besides, Luca didn't know English. How would he manage to understand orders and do his job if he didn't know the language? He'd better learn it and learn it fast if he wanted to keep his job. Will wasn't about to call Giulio to interpret every time Will wanted to talk with Luca. Giulio had his own job to do, and taking time away from that job would cost Will money. Major money.

Not to mention the wrath of Oliver Cramdon.

Worst of all, Will didn't like the way Paulina had looked at the new employee. The way she'd sized him up with her eyes.

And her emotions.

Will recognized that look, and he wanted it all for himself. Had had it all for himself for a good while now.

Until today.

In fact, for the last several months he'd kept Paulina on the side for his own personal satisfaction.

Not that she minded, of course.

But they'd had to keep things on the hush-hush. Without catching the attention of Cramdon and his crew at headquarters.

Nor of Will's employees at the workshop.

It hadn't been easy. So far, all was going well. Things seemed to be moving right along. Will had even thought of asking Paulina to marry him one day.

Until Luca Tonetta's arrival.

Will's chest burned. It didn't take much for a woman like Paulina to switch her allegiance, and to switch it fast. He certainly wasn't a stranger to female fickleness.

And he didn't like it one bit.

The next time they were alone, he'd take her to task on her wretched behavior. When it came to women, Will had never been one to like competition of any kind. For him, it was all or nothing.

And he preferred to keep it that way.

He'd make sure Luca Tonetta stayed away from his woman. It didn't matter that Tonetta was married. Will had seen enough hanky-panky among the immigrants not to trust anyone. One mistake on the Italian tailor's part, and he'd be out of the picture for good.

Will stood and walked to the window. The twin Gothic-style towers of the Brooklyn Bridge hovered high above him, so close he could almost touch them. Towers of strength he'd heard them called. They were made of granite and limestone and laced with thick steel cables. Strikingly beautiful.

And a perfect backdrop for ending it all.

He turned back toward his desk and sat down. It was getting more and more difficult to push back the suicidal thoughts that increasingly bombarded him. He had to stay strong.

But for whose sake? Whom did he have who cared about him?

He placed his elbows on his desk and buried his face in his hands. A pang speared his soul. Katie was gone. Willie was gone. Mama was gone. There was no one out there who cared whether he lived or died.

Why should *he* care?

He shook his head. No. Luca Tonetta was not going to

work out as planned.

But Will needed a legitimate reason to get rid of him. A reason that went beyond his own personal dislike of the man.

Beyond his worry over Paulina's possible defection.

Even beyond his own personal prejudice against Italians.

Will raised his head and chuckled. Mama would be glad he still had an ounce of decency left in his bones. She'd tried so hard to raise him right. Not a small feat, raising a boisterous son without his father.

The bum. He'd upped and left Will and Mama one rainy night and never returned. Will was barely out of diapers.

Never heard from the old man again.

He swallowed hard. He'd promised he'd never be that kind of father to his own son. Yet, God had taken away Will's only chance to prove himself different from his father.

What kind of God would do that?

Not a God worth serving.

Will sorted through the pile of papers on his desk and found a letter from Oliver Cramdon. Why did every communication from Cramdon make his stomach roil? The old man kept wanting more and more.

More garments. More workers to make the garments. More work hours from those workers.

More profit.

That was it. The money.

It was always about the money. A never-ending drive for more money.

Greed, his Irish mother used to call it, God rest her soul.

Greed will kill ye, my boy. Run from it! Will could still hear her voice ringing in his ten-year-old ears.

A lump formed at the back of his throat. Losing Mama when he was fourteen nearly rivaled losing Katie and little Will.

Was life about only loss and pain? Only suffering and

then dying?

He choked back the tears that stung his eyes. No self-respecting man should be caught crying.

But then again, he hadn't respected himself since Katie and little Will had died. It was then the drinking had begun.

The debauchery.

The despair.

With shaky hands, he broke open the seal on Cramdon's letter and unfolded the crinkled sheet of paper. On it his boss had listed the due dates for delivery of garments in time for Christmas retail distribution. Each retail store was listed by name, along with the number of garments ordered.

Will studied the list. The first batch of fifteen hundred garments was due in two short weeks. Will raked his fingers through his hair. Reaching that goal would require overtime on the part of every one of his employees every day for the entire two weeks. They might even have to work on weekends. There was no way his workers could finish that many garments on their normal work schedule with such short notice.

Will cursed under his breath and folded the letter. He'd have to go back to the workshop now to relay Cramdon's orders. There was no time to lose.

And he'd have to keep Luca Tonetta on the job.

He swallowed the bile that rose to his throat.

As he walked down the hall from his office toward the workshop, Paulina walked out of the ladies' room.

She smiled at him and proceeded toward the workshop, accentuating the femaleness of her stride.

She had a way of conveying what was on her mind without saying a word.

He smiled in return and followed her toward the workshop, admiring her beautiful blonde tresses and the way they fell over her shapely shoulders.

He hoped it wouldn't be long before he'd be with her

again.

If he weren't her boss, he could be open about things. He might even ask her to marry him. God knew he could use some companionship.

He reached the workshop door just as she did. "May I?" He opened the door for her.

"Why, thank you, Mr. Dempsey."

He appreciated the way she always referred to him by his last name when they were at work, in case there were any flies on the wall to spy on them. When they were alone, it was another matter.

He laughed. "My mama didn't raise no bum. She raised a gentleman."

As he spoke the words, a twinge of guilt assailed him. Gentlemen didn't hang out at bars and spend their week's paycheck on liquor. Gentlemen didn't get drunk and drop into gutters on a Saturday night, only to be dragged home by the police.

Gentlemen didn't chase loose women like Paulina for their own gratification.

Will drew in a deep breath.

Maybe Mama had raised a bum after all.

* * * *

His insides churning, Luca returned home at the end of his first day on the new job. Working only on parts of a garment rather than the whole garment had proven quite frustrating. One of the things he loved about tailoring was working on the entire garment from start to finish and seeing the final results. But his new job required only that he work on the sleeves of every garment and that he repeat the same process over and over, countless times. Piecework they called it, and, frankly, Luca did not like it one bit. The repetitive process bored him and did not provide the satisfaction he used to experience at taking a garment from start to finish.

Releasing a long breath, he opened the door to his flat and greeted Maria and the children.

"Papa! Papa! You're home!" Valeria and Anna rushed to greet him, wrapping their little arms around his legs.

Nico lifted his eyes from the book he was reading and offered a smile of welcome from across the room. "Hello, Papa."

Invigorated by their presence, Luca greeted his family with a smile.

Maria approached and gave him a hug. "Well, how was your first day of work?"

Luca collapsed into a nearby chair and wiped his hand across his brow. "It's a lot different from owning my own shop—that's for sure." He managed a weak smile.

Maria drew up a chair next to him. "You look unhappy."

"I'm fine. It just takes a little getting used to, that's all." He did not want to tell her that the worst part of his day had been contending with that wicked woman Paulina. She was up to no good with her flirtatious eyes, her seductive smile, and her constant conversation about things that no decent woman should talk about. Tomorrow he would ask Will to be switched to another workstation.

Maria placed her hand on his. "You must be hungry. I made *pasta e fagioli*."

Nico rose and mumbled. "Oh, Mama. I'm getting tired of pasta and beans. We've had it three nights in a row."

Luca gave him a stern look. "Be thankful, Nico. Some children are going to bed hungry tonight."

The boy's gaze dropped to the floor. "I'm sorry, Papa."

"I forgive you." Luca rose. "Now, let's eat."

Luca pulled the small rectangular table away from the wall and set it in the center of the narrow room. Then he arranged the five wooden chairs around it. As Maria and the children took their places around the table, his heart filled with gratitude. "Let's pray. Father God, we thank You for all that You have provided for us. I thank You for my job that allows me to take care of my family. I thank You for this food that You have provided for us. Thank You for my precious wife who prepared it, and thank You for my beautiful children who partake of it. Strengthen us, Father, to do Your will as we focus on serving You day by day and spreading Your truth and Your love wherever we go. In Jesus' Name we pray. Amen."

Valeria and Anna shouted "Amen!"

Nico mumbled a weak "Amen" under his breath.

Luca shot a worried glance toward his son but remained silent. Luca would have to have a talk with him later to find out what was going on inside him.

Maria took Luca's plate and placed a large portion of *pasta e fagioli* on it. "*Mangia.* You need your strength." She then served Nico, Valeria, and Anna. Finally, she took a small portion for herself.

Luca addressed the children. "Tell me what you did today."

Anna's face lit up. "I played with my doll. She took a nap and then I fed her." His youngest daughter's delight warmed Luca's heart. "And what about you, Valeria?"

"I helped Anna play with her doll."

Luca burst into laughter. "Playing often requires the help of another, doesn't it?" The entire family joined in the laughter.

"And Nico? What did you do today?"

"I went outside and met some of the boys from the neighborhood."

Luca looked up, attentive to discern anything that might be amiss. "Were they *americani*?"

"Some were, Papa, but most of them were *siciliani* like

us."

"So you were able to converse with them."

Nico nodded. "They all have jobs."

"Really? How old are they? And what kind of work do they do?"

"One sweeps the streets at night; two work in factories as delivery boys; one works on the railroads."

"I see." What was Nico getting at? Luca ate slowly and waited for his son to continue.

"May I get a job, too, Papa?"

Yes. That was what Nico was getting at. Luca looked at his son. "But you are only eleven years old. Besides, I want you to go to school. I want you to learn English so you can contribute to your new homeland. I want you to get educated so you can have a better life than your Mama and I."

"The boys I met are not much older than I am, Papa. One of them is twelve; the other three are fourteen."

Luca glanced at Maria. Her eyes were wide with concern. "Don't you think you should play with boys your own age?"

"I'm almost twelve, papa. Besides, I don't know any boys my age around here."

Maria intervened. "I have been praying that you meet boys your age from good families."

Nico furrowed his brows. "Are you saying, Mama, that the boys I met do not come from good families?"

"I am not saying that at all, but, frankly, I don't know for sure. Teenage boys should not be hanging out on street corners, smoking cigarettes. They should be in school, learning to be responsible citizens."

Luca studied his son. The boy's eyes had lost their spark, and his demeanor had become lethargic. Ever since the incident with Nico's dog and Luca's decision to leave the pup behind in Sicily, Nico had grown distant. Disinterested.

Discouraged.

"If I go to work, Papa, I can help support the family. So we don't have to eat *pasta e fagioli* every night."

Luca put his spoon down, his stomach in a tight knot. "Nico, it is not your job to support the family. It is mine. It is your job to obey me and to do what I say. And I said I want you to go to school. We came to this country so we can have a better life. Part of a better life for my children is getting a good education. Here you can go to school free of charge. I want you to take advantage of that opportunity."

Nico kept his eyes glued to the floor. "Yes, Papa."

Luca picked up his spoon again. "I spoke with some people at work today about how to enroll you in the public school here in our neighborhood. They told me what to do."

Maria turned toward him. "What did they say?"

"All we have to do is go down to the school with some-one who speaks English and fill out the necessary papers. Once the papers are processed, Nico can begin attending, possibly as soon as next week."

Maria placed a hand on Luca's arm. "But who will come with us to interpret?"

"I've already asked Giulio. He said he would be happy to accompany us."

"May I go to school, too, Papa?" Valeria piped up from the other side of the table.

Luca chuckled. "When you are old enough, you, too, may go to school."

Valeria clapped her hands and turned to Anna. "Do you want to go to school with me, Anna?"

Anna gave an enthusiastic nod of her head. "Anna go to school, too!"

Luca laughed. "That settles it then. All of my children will go to school and contribute to our new homeland. Who knows? One of you may become a doctor. Another a lawyer."

Nico spoke. "What's wrong with being a tailor?"

Luca looked at him. "There is absolutely nothing wrong with being a tailor, son. All labor is respectable when one does it for the Lord. Even a doctor could displease God if he works for his own gain and cares nothing about honoring the Lord in his work."

Nico pushed his plate away. "Can we open a tailor shop, Papa?"

Hope rushed through Luca's heart. "The thought has crossed my mind."

"It has?" Nico's gaze was fast upon him.

"Yes, especially after today." Instantly, Luca regretted uttering the words.

Maria shot him a questioning look.

Luca ignored it. "I still want you to go to school, Nico. Then, after you graduate from high school, if you are still interested in owning a tailoring business, you will have my blessing."

A thin smile lined Nico's lips.

Maria was on Luca. "What happened today?"

Luca studied his precious wife. Dark circles clouded her eyes. "Perhaps we can talk later, when the children are asleep."

"Very well." Maria rose from the table.

Luca rose, too. "Here, let me help you clean up."

When the kitchen was cleaned and the children were fast asleep, Luca sat down with Maria at the kitchen table. He took her hands in his. "What is troubling you, Sweetheart? I can see in your eyes that something is not right."

Maria squeezed his hands. "I am worried about Mama. I wrote to Cristina the day after we arrived and am finding it extremely difficult to wait almost two months for a reply. I am worried that Mama might have died at the port."

An arrow pierced Luca's heart. "I have been concerned, too. But there is nothing we can do except pray and wait. We have been here only a week, so it will be a while before your letter reaches Cristina and her response reaches you."

"Yes. But the waiting is so difficult." Her gaze was fixed on him. "Luca, do you think we made a mistake leaving Sicily?"

He lowered his head. He had to be honest with her. "I cannot lie to you. That thought has gone through my mind many times. But we left trusting that God was leading us. We must continue to trust He is leading us."

A tear trickled down her cheek.

He cupped her hands in his. "Perhaps when you make some friends, it will be easier for you. We can invite them over for dinner."

Maria burst into tears. "Luca, we barely have enough room for our own family to eat, let alone enough space to accommodate guests."

Luca's heart broke. How difficult it must be for his wife to be confined to a single room after living her whole live in a spacious villa with several large rooms. What had he done to her? "Maria, I promise you that one day you will have a house of your own."

She withdrew her hands from his and rose, her face turning red. "I had a house of my own. A beautiful house that I agreed to leave behind. I don't want another house of my own. I want *Bella Terra*. That is the only house I ever wanted and the only house I will ever want."

Luca raked his fingers through his hair. What was going on? After a week in their new homeland, Maria had seemed to be adjusting well. This surprising turn of events was not something he'd expected.

Luca rose to take her into his arms, but she escaped his embrace.

She started to run away but stopped. There was no place to run. Burying her face in her hands, she fell on the bed and wept.

Luca knelt on the floor beside her and prayed.

Chapter Eleven

Long after Maria fell asleep, Luca prayed. He prayed far into the night and into the wee hours of the morning. By the time he crawled into bed, it was almost time to get up for work.

Maria's unexpected outburst the night before had sent him reeling to the edge of despair. Surely they could not continue well if she persisted in her negative attitude. He tried to be understanding, but at some point, she would just have to accept their situation and make the best of it.

As the dawn light filtered through the balcony door, Luca tossed and turned. The prospect of another day in the workshop unnerved him. He would ask Will, first thing, to move him to another station.

But what reason could he give?

If he told Will the truth, Will would accuse him of judging Paulina. If Luca said nothing, he'd have to endure endless days of this woman's wicked behavior.

Of course, the best option would be to tell her about Jesus so she would be born again. That would end her flirtation for sure. But would Paulina listen to him? Only if he tried would he find out.

Luca wanted very much to ask Maria's opinion. But with all she already had on her mind, he didn't want to burden her with yet another worry.

At the first sign of sunlight, he rose and walked over to the balcony door. The sky was a different color here in America. Not the deep, rich blue he'd known in Sicily. Instead, it had a perpetual gray cast—even on good days— probably the result of the many factories spitting fumes into the air.

His mind drifted back to the beautiful sunrises he'd experienced in Pisano. Each morning, when he'd open the shutters of his shop, the brilliant sun lifted over the purple mountains, greeting him with its morning smile.

He swallowed hard. Jesus warned against thinking of the past. It was behind them now. Gone forever.

Only the future remained.

But what sort of future? Would it be a future better than the past?

His heart heavy, Luca turned to get washed and dressed for work. The day before, Will had informed the employees that, for the next two weeks, they would have to work overtime. This meant reporting to work at six o'clock in the morning and working until the day's quota was reached. Whatever that quota might be. Only God knew what time he'd be home.

He left a note for Maria, informing her that he would have to work late. That done, he grabbed a piece of bread and a chunk of cheese and wrapped them in brown paper. Then, leaning over a sleeping Maria, he kissed her gently on the forehead.

She stirred but did not awaken.

His heart warmed. She needed all the rest she could get.

Thank God he had only to walk up a flight of stairs to get to work. So many of his fellow immigrants had to catch trains and buses or walk long distances to their places of employment.

As he entered the stairwell, his body tensed. Just a few steps ahead of him, Paulina was climbing the stairs.

She turned and smiled. "Why, good morning!"

He forced a smile. "Good morning!"

"Do you live in this tenement house, too?"

He had a sudden urge to run. "Yes. I did not know you

live in this building."

"Actually, I live on the sixth floor, but I had to go down to report a plumbing problem to the janitor." She waited for Luca to join her on her step. "If you ever need to report a problem with your flat, the janitor's office is on the first floor, near the main entrance to the building."

"Thank you." Luca motioned for her to go ahead and waited while she continued up the stairs. He lowered his eyes to avoid watching her swinging hips as she climbed.

When she reached the top, she smiled and waited for him to open the door for her.

His muscles tensed at being in the stairwell alone with her. Ever since becoming a Christian, he had made sure never to give the appearance of evil. Even when he'd hired Maria to work for him in Pisano before they were married, he'd wanted her to work from home.

And she did.

After his single fall from grace upon the tragic death of his parents and before he'd accepted Christ, he vowed never again to put himself in a compromising situation with a woman.

Now, against his will, here he was in a compromising situation. *Lord, help me.*

He opened the door and allowed Paulina to enter before him.

"May I get you a cup of coffee before we start the day?"

"No, thank you. I'll get my own."

"Very well. Have it your way."

No. Not his way. God's way. The only way that would keep him pure.

The only way that mattered in life.

After Paulina had gotten her coffee, Luca walked over to the coffee pot.

Jake Goldberg came up beside him, smiling broadly. The man was always so positive and uplifting. "Good morning, Luca!"

"Good morning, Jake!"

"So, my friend, how was your first day of work?"

Luca took a sip of his coffee. "Not bad."

"You do outstanding work. I watched you yesterday. You are a true professional."

Luca smiled. "Thank you. You are quite an excellent tailor yourself."

Jake laughed. "*Danke.* My father taught me everything I know. When other little boys were out playing ball, I was at my father's knees, learning how to tailor. He worried that I needed to learn a trade if I wanted to survive."

"You sound like my father with me and now me with my son Nico. He used to work with me back in my tailor shop in Sicily. I'd hoped he would take over my business one day."

"But life got in the way, right?"

Luca really liked Jake. He had depth. More depth than met the eye. "Yes, life got in the way."

Jake placed a hand on Luca's shoulder. "I understand, my friend." He withdrew his hand. "So you are from Sicily. A beautiful place. I went there on holiday once with my parents. I was eight years old, but I still remember the brightly dressed donkeys." Jake chuckled.

"Yes, they are big tourist attractions. I've often felt sorry for the poor beasts, covered over with those heavy blankets in the hot weather."

Jake nodded. "I hear you, my friend. I would not like to be one of those donkeys." He laughed a laugh straight from his heart. "I myself am from Germany. A bit colder land, *ja?*" He smiled. "From a small town just south of Frankfurt called Darmstadt. Have you ever been to Germany?"

"Actually, I was there once on business. I brought back a

beautiful clock that I left with my mother-in-law in Sicily."

"So, you've seen my beautiful homeland." The nostalgia in Jake's voice touched Luca's heart. Jake understood.

Luca accompanied Jake to their worktable. "How long have you been in America?"

"Fourteen years. I came as a young lad of sixteen with my parents and two brothers." Jake sighed. "My parents have since died, but my brothers are still alive. One lives in Manhattan and the other went to seek his fortune in the western part of the country. I opted to remain in Brooklyn." He winked at Luca. "Good thing I did. I met my beautiful wife here. A native of Germany as well. In fact, she is from Frankfurt."

"How providential!"

Jake's gaze locked with Luca's, as though searching his soul. "Yes." Jake's voice softened. "Providential, indeed."

Luca felt a special kinship with this man. He liked him. Liked him a lot. With his ever-present black *yarmulke* on his head, his lively sense of humor, and his warm smile, Jake inspired Luca with his positive outlook on life. Yes. Jake could become a good friend.

"Well, we'd better get to work before Mr. Dempsey finds us looking idle." Jake patted Luca's shoulder. "Will Dempsey is a man you do not want to cross." Jake led the way to the workstation. When they arrived, Paulina was already seated and busy at her sewing machine, as was Gennaro.

"*Guten Morgen*, Paulina. Gennaro." Jake placed his coffee cup on the table beside his sewing machine.

Gennaro nodded and smiled in reply.

"*Buon giorno*, Jake." Paulina acknowledged him.

Jake pulled out his chair and sat down. "We have a long day ahead of us. A large quota of garments to complete. We must keep our conversation to a minimum."

That was fine with Luca. The less he had to talk with Paulina, the better.

Luca took his place at his workstation. At the first sign of Mr. Dempsey, Luca would ask to be moved to another workstation.

* * * *

While Valeria and Anna played with their dolls, Maria stared out the door that led to the balcony. Not since the horrific incident with Don Franco had she felt so discouraged. So depressed.

So hopeless.

A gray sky hung low over the long row of run-down tenement houses that lined both sides of the narrow street. Balconies with wrought-iron railings hung precariously from the buildings, laden with laundry hung out to dry. Rusted fire escapes snaked down the walls between the balconies, providing a way to safety should the need arise.

She clutched her chest. She'd been in Brooklyn only a week and already that need to escape had arisen in her heart. To escape the confinement of the tiny, narrow flat. The stark loneliness of being among crowds of people but still feeling isolated.

The emptiness of having no one to talk to all day except the children. With Luca gone twelve to fourteen hours a day, she felt like a widow.

If only she could return to the beloved homeland she'd left behind.

Her mind drifted to Mama. The agony of not knowing what had happened to her after she'd fainted at the port only added to Maria's anguish. She would have to wait another month before receiving a response from her sister Cristina.

A knock at the door startled her. She stiffened. Who could be calling? Should she open the door? How would she respond if the person did not speak Italian?

Valeria rose to open the door.

"No, Valeria!" Maria grabbed her little girl by the hand. "Mama will open the door."

Smoothing her apron with the palms of her hands, Maria walked toward the door. At the sound of the second knock, she opened it.

A middle-aged woman with graying hair at the temples greeted her with a smile. *"Buon giorno."*

Relief flooded Maria's soul. The woman spoke Italian. "Good day to you, too."

"I'm sorry for intruding, but I noticed you and your family when you moved in last week. I wanted to welcome you to our tenement house and to give you this." She handed Maria a loaf of bread, still warm from the oven.

"Why, thank you!"

"You are most welcome. My name is Enza. Enza Addevico."

Maria smiled in return. "Pleased to meet you, Enza. My name is Maria Tonetta. Please. Won't you come in?"

Enza entered the tiny apartment.

Maria pointed to each of her children. "This is Valeria, and this is Anna. Children, say hello to our neighbor, *Signora* Addevico."

"Ciao," the two little girls chimed in unison. Then they returned to playing with their dolls.

Maria motioned toward the table. "Do you have time for a cup of espresso?"

"Actually, I do have a few moments. But only a few. My children return from school in half an hour, and I like to be there when they arrive."

"Of course." Maria quickly set up a pot of espresso and then joined Enza at the table. "So you, too, are Italian. I am so glad. I have been nervous to venture out because I do not speak English."

Enza smiled. "You will learn soon enough. In fact, if your children are like mine, they will learn before you do and then teach you." Enza laughed, with a laugh that warmed Maria's heart.

"Do you live on this floor?" Maria studied the woman's kind eyes.

"Yes. I live two doors down, across the hall. I'm sorry I have not visited before now."

"No, please. It is so kind of you to stop by today."

"Well, I remember how lonely I felt when I first arrived from Italy."

The coffee pot sputtered. Maria rose to turn off the flame. She took two demi-tasse cups from the cupboard and placed them on the table. Then she stirred some sugar into the coffee pot and brought it to the table. She poured some espresso into both of the demi-tasse cups then sat down. "So, Enza, tell me about you. From what part of Italy do you hail?"

Enza's eyes lit up. "From Napoli, the most beautiful city in the world."

Maria admired the enthusiasm with which her new friend described her native city. "Do you miss it?"

Enza's eyes filled with tears. "There is an old saying that goes like this: *Vedi Napoli e poi muori! See Naples, and then die.* After one has seen Naples, one is ready to die because there is nothing more beautiful left to see."

A lump formed in Maria's throat. "I understand exactly what you mean. I feel the same way about Sicily, especially the area in which I grew up."

"There is no place like Italy for its natural beauty, but—" Enza leaned toward Maria as though about to divulge a confidence—"there is no place like America for opportunity to succeed."

Enza inspired trust, a trust Maria had been longing for ever since her arrival in her new homeland. "I hope you are right. I have had my doubts since we arrived."

"Trust me. I have been here ten years already. When I first arrived, I was heart-broken and missed Italy terribly, especially my family. But we would never have survived there. The economy was in a shambles; the unemployment rate was high; and an education cost a fortune. Here, my husband has a good, well-paying job; our income is three times what it was in Italy; and my children are getting a good education. This is truly the land of opportunity."

Maria's heart lightened. "What kind of work does your husband do?"

"He is a plumber. He learned the trade here and has done quite well in it. For a man who, in Italy, could not clean a drain, he has done quite well for himself."

Maria laughed—the first deep laugh she'd had since reaching American shores.

Enza continued. "If you ever have a problem with your pipes—and I hope you never do—you know whom to call."

"Thank you. By the way, how old are your children?"

"I have a fourteen-year-old daughter named Gina, a twelve-year-old son named Dominic, and an eight-year-old daughter named Lia."

Maria's heart leapt at the thought of a possible friend for Nico. "I have my two little girls—Valeria who is four and Anna who is two—and I have an eleven-year-old son named Nico. He's been quite lonely since we arrived. He is outside right now. He's met a few boys from the neighborhood, but I am concerned about the quality of their influence on him."

"Yes, you do have to be careful. Some of the boys here are a bit—how shall I say?—rebellious. But your son must meet my Dominic. He is a good boy, if I do say so myself." Enza chuckled.

"Yes, I would very much like Nico to meet Dominic. Perhaps you can bring him with you next time you come."

"I will do that." Enza swallowed the last drop of her espresso and then rose. "But now, I must be getting back to my flat. The children will be arriving momentarily, and if they don't find me home, they will worry."

Maria rose, too. "I cannot thank you enough for stopping by. You have no idea what your visit has meant to me."

Enza patted Maria's hand. "Oh, believe me—I do." She smiled warmly and turned to go.

Maria prompted her children. "Say goodbye to *Signora* Addevico."

"*Ciao, Signora* Addevico."

"*Ciao*, little ones. Have fun playing with your dollies."

Maria walked Enza to the door. "Thank you for the homemade bread. We will enjoy it with thanksgiving at dinner this evening."

"Oh, don't even mention it. Thank you for the delicious espresso." Enza gave Maria a hug. "We Italians must stick together."

Maria nodded. Enza was right. In a strange land, Italians must stick together.

* * * *

It was early afternoon by the time Will Dempsey made his first appearance of the day on the busy workshop floor. Amid the incessant whirring of sewing machines and the cacophonous buzz of ceiling fans spinning wildly on this unusually warm October day, Luca had been awaiting his boss's arrival with eagerness and trepidation, all the while resisting the seductive advances of the woman seated across from him. Paulina was an unwelcome distraction he neither needed nor wanted.

The sooner he switched workstations, the better.

Praying silently for wisdom, Luca concentrated on the ladies' jacket sleeve he was sewing. Already that day he'd sewn forty of them and then passed them on to the next workstation, where tailors and seamstresses attached the sleeves to the bodices of the jackets. Why couldn't each person sew a complete jacket? It would make the work much more interesting and so much less monotonous. And it would give each worker a sense of satisfaction at seeing his job completed. This American way of piecemeal sewing robbed the trade of its art.

Luca was about to get up to stretch a moment when Will pushed through the main doors, his face flushed, his gait a bit unsteady.

Luca settled back into his chair, removed his foot from the treadle, and lifted his gaze from his sewing machine. At the sight of Will, his muscles tensed.

His boss looked angry. Broken.

Worried.

For an instant, Luca felt a twinge of compassion for him.

Will headed straight for Luca's table. The look on Will's face boded problems.

Luca waited, his thoughts spinning.

Will leaned both hands on Luca's end of the table and scanned the four workers stationed there. "Just heard from Cramdon." The smell of whiskey was on Will's breath. "He's doubled our quota to three thousand garments by the end of two weeks." His gaze went off into space.

Luca's heart sank. Already they'd been scheduled to work fourteen-hour days, six days a week. How could they possibly do double the work in the same amount of time?

Will straightened. "We're going to have to work Sundays in order to get the job done."

Luca's heart lurched. Sundays. Sunday was the Lord's Day. The day Luca took Maria and the children to church.

The Bible forbade working on the Sabbath.

And so did the Blue Laws. Giulio had told Luca about them.

Luca wished he had an interpreter. He shook his head and mumbled the few words he'd learned since arriving. "No. No work Sunday."

Will's eyes became slits. He waved a hand in front of Luca's face. "No work Sunday, no job Monday!"

Desperate to explain, Luca turned toward Gennaro to interpret for him. "Please explain to Mr. Dempsey that I cannot work on Sundays because it is the Lord's Day."

At Gennaro's translation, Paulina raised an eyebrow, as though Luca were from another planet.

The veins in Will's forehead nearly broke through his skin. His eyes narrowed as he glared at Luca. "Either you work when I tell you to work, or you won't work at all." His voice rose to high decibels.

Luca could not back down and still obey his Lord. "Then I will have to quit." He couldn't believe the words had come out of his mouth. If he quit, he'd be out of a job, with no means of supporting his family.

The look of surprise on Will's face gave Luca the upper hand. Obviously, Will had expected Luca to cave in. Now Will would be saddled with one fewer employee to reach Cramdon's quota.

It was called leverage, and Luca had it.

Will stared at Luca. "Maybe we could work out a compromise."

"What sort of compromise?"

"How about you work two extra hours a day—that's twelve extra hours a week—to make up for the twelve you would work on Sundays?"

Luca's heart clenched. Sixteen hours a day. He'd never get to see Maria and the children. Plus, how could he work sixteen hours a day, six days a week, on only a few hours of sleep per night?

"I will have to think about this, Mr. Dempsey. Not even animals work that long and that hard."

Gennaro interpreted Luca's words to Will. From the hesitant tone of Gennaro's voice, Luca could tell he didn't think Luca's response was an appropriate one. If, that is, he wanted to keep his job.

Will turned on Luca. "I want your answer by closing time today. If I don't get it, you're fired. Do you hear me?"

Without waiting for a reply, Will stormed out of the workroom, slamming the door behind him.

Luca let out a long breath. So much for asking his boss to move him to another workstation.

Chapter Twelve

Back in his office, Will Dempsey collapsed into his swivel chair. Between the effects of the liquor on his body and the effects of Luca's resistance on his soul, Will needed a nap.

A long nap.

He blew out a long breath of air and raked his fingers through his hair. No, he needed more than a nap.

He needed to end it all.

His stomach muscles tightened at the memory of Paulina giving Luca the eye. And it hadn't been the evil eye. The fickle woman. He and Paulina had been together for seven months now, and already she had her eyes on another man.

A married man.

The nerve. At least Will was a widower.

His jaw twitched. He'd believed her when she'd said she loved him.

It was all his fault for trusting her in the first place.

As if the situation with Paulina weren't enough of a headache, Cramdon's orders to double the quota to three thousand garments in two weeks overwhelmed him. Had the man gone crazy? Cramdon had no clue about what was involved in producing garments. The last time he'd visited the shop was when it first opened seven years earlier. Since then, he'd sat in his ivory tower office overlooking the East River, sipping coffee and counting his money.

Money made at the expense of someone else's blood, sweat, and tears.

Will swiveled his chair toward the window. Covered with gray clouds, the Brooklyn Bridge towered before him, ominous and strong.

And inviting.

A good jump from its railing could end it all. No wonder Francis McCarey, a drunk like Will, had jumped off of it and died four years earlier in 1892. Will could relate to the man's need to prove he was somebody. Others had attempted the same jump, with some dying and some surviving.

What would happen to him if he jumped? Would his attempt succeed or fail?

Probably fail. Just like everything else in his life.

But there was only one way to find out....

He turned back toward his desk, his thoughts shifting to Luca. The tailor's refusal to work on Sundays had gotten stuck in Will's craw. Truth be told, despite his anger at Luca, his employee's adamant stance had inspired Will's respect. Not something he could say for all of his workers.

Will leaned back in his chair. Not many people these days honored God the way Luca did. But why? Why would Luca risk his job for a God Who didn't care? After all the man had a wife and three kids to support. Not like Will, who had only himself to think about.

A pang of remorse speared his soul. What had happened to him? To the little boy in whom his Mama had believed? He closed his eyes, picturing Mama Dempsey in all her glory.

"Now, Willie." She held him tight and shook a stern finger at him while her eyes glowed with love. "You're my boy, and don't you ever forget that. One day you'll grow up to be a fine man, a man who loves God and loves his neighbor. Always obey God and do the right thing, you hear? It's never foolish to obey God."

Willie squirmed out of her embrace. Mama was dreaming her silly dreams again. Willie wanted nothing to do with her God. Her God had given him a mean daddy, one who came home drunk every night and beat him to a pulp just for being alive. Then the old man would start on Mama. Nor did Willie care a wit about any neighbor. All the neighbors did was complain about Daddy and the horrible way he shouted at Mama whenever he was home.

Will squinted and brushed aside the tear that trickled from his eye. *Get a grip, Dempsey! You're a grown man now. What happened to you as a kid is over and done with. No need to go messin' around in the past again.*

A knock on the door interrupted his misery. "Come in!" He shouted more loudly than he'd intended to.

The door opened slowly. Luca entered, followed by Giulio, and closed the door behind him. "Mr. Dempsey, may I speak with you?"

Will motioned to the empty chair across from his desk. "Sit down."

Luca sat down while Giulio stood to his side, ready to interpret.

Will pointed a finger at Luca. "You'd better learn English soon."

Giulio jumped in. "He is working on it, Mr. Dempsey."

"Good. Now, what do you want?"

Luca glanced at Giulio for understanding. "I want to tell you that if you continue to insist I work on Sundays, I will quit now."

Will leaned forward and looked Luca straight in the eye. "Do you realize what you're doing? If you quit, you won't have any money to support your wife and children."

"I am fully aware of that."

"But you're being crazy! Irresponsible! What in the world could prompt you to act so foolishly?"

"It is never foolish to obey God."

Luca's words hit Will squarely in the chest. They were Mama's words. Will swallowed hard, remembering them well. A shudder coursed through his veins. "But surely God can't be telling you to neglect your family?"

"If I obey God, He will take care of my family."

Luca's determination made Will's blood boil. "But how can you be so sure?"

Luca smiled. "I know my God."

A twinge of envy struck Will's heart. Could he know God in the same way that Luca knew Him? Did Will even want to? "By rights, I should fire you. But I'm not going to. I'm going to give you the option of working extra hours on six days and taking off on Sundays to go to church. Now, it's up to you if you want that option."

"Yes. I do want it. I will accept your offer and trust God to take care of the rest."

Will nodded. "Fine. That's all. You can get back to work now."

"Thank you, Mr. Dempsey. Thank you very much." Luca rose and turned to go.

Will stood. "Tonetta, wait a minute."

"Yes?"

"Your Mama taught you well."

Luca smiled. "Thank you, Mr. Dempsey. I have a feeling your Mama taught you well, too."

Will pushed back the lump that rose to his throat. He nodded, unable to speak the unfamiliar remorse that now filled his soul.

* * * *

The late-afternoon sun burned hot on Maria's head despite the decreasing temperatures of early October. Her new American neighbors called it an "Indian Summer" day— an unusually warm day for this time of year. To her delight, she was beginning to learn a few words of English, a feat that had seemed well nigh impossible only a few short weeks ago.

She held Valeria's and Anna's hands as they walked through the open-air Italian market one block from their tenement house. Finding herself among fellow Italians bolstered her spirits and renewed her hope. These were her people who, like her, had left their native Italy to find new opportunities for their families. They had adapted well. She would adapt well.

"*Buon giorno, Signora Tonetta!*" Alessandro the produce-vendor gave her a big smile. "I have some fresh eggplant this morning, straight from my uncle's farm in New Jersey." He picked up an eggplant. "Look at the beautiful purple color. Doesn't it make your mouth water? Imagine eggplant *alla parmigiana* cooked with this."

Maria laughed. "All right. You've convinced me. I'll take two of them."

He chose two beautiful specimens of eggplant, placed them in a paper bag, and handed them to Maria. "That will be twenty-five cents, please."

She gave him a sidelong glance. "Alessandro, I'm a *paesana*. A countryman. Can you make it twenty cents?"

He hesitated, but only for a brief moment. "All right. Twenty cents for my *paesana* from Italy."

"Grazie!" She reached into her purse, counted out the payment, and handed it to him with a big smile.

He took it from her and handed her the bag of eggplant in exchange.

"Enjoy the rest of your day," Maria said over her shoulder as she took her daughters' hands once again and headed back toward home. For the first time since her arrival in America, she was starting to feel happy and hopeful. Luca would be home from work soon, and she wanted to prepare him a special meal, not only because the poor man was exhausted from the long hours he'd been working, but also because she wanted to make up for her ungodly attitude the last several days. She hadn't acted like the devoted follower of Christ she'd claimed to be.

A lump formed in her throat as she whispered a prayer of repentance. How thankful she was that all she had to do was sincerely confess her sin and God was faithful to forgive her.

"Mama, I'm hungry." Valeria tugged on Maria's hand.

"I am, too, Mama."

Maria laughed. Little Anna mimicked her older sister in everything. Just as her own sister Cristina used to do with her.

The thought of Cristina, Luciana, and Mama back in Sicily triggered an alarm in her soul. Any day now a letter should arrive from Cristina informing her of Mama's health. Maria's stomach tightened. Was Mama all right? Was she still alive?

Before the fearful thoughts could grab hold of her mind, Maria pushed them aside and entrusted them to the Lord. Turning the corner toward her tenement house, she spotted Nico talking with a group of boys his age. Her nerves went on high alert. The boys were smoking cigarettes and seemed up to no good.

"Nico! Nico! Come here!"

Her voice caught his attention. He turned, left the boys standing on the street corner, and ran toward her. When he reached her, he was out of breath. "Yes, Mama?"

Maria studied her son's face. He was rapidly changing from a little boy to a young man. He'd grown considerably in height, and his voice had lowered a notch. Soon he would be twelve years old, the age at which she and Luca had agreed to tell him about his birth father. Her heart tightened. "Who are those boys?"

Nico looked back toward his friends. "Oh, just some boys who live in the neighborhood."

Maria's gaze shifted toward the boys. They were looking

her way with smirks on their faces. "But they are smoking, and they look about your age."

"Two of them are twelve and one is fourteen."

Maria squared her jaw. "Don't you ever let me catch you smoking—do you hear me?"

He lowered his head. "Yes, Mama."

"Smoking is a dirty habit, one that will harm your body and, worst of all, harm your soul."

Nico nodded and then raised his head. "Mama, do you think I'll ever have any friends?"

A lump rose to the back of Maria's throat. "I'm sure you will. In fact, I'd like you to meet Enza Addevico's son Dominic. He is a good boy and lives down the hall from us. I think you will like him."

Nico remained silent.

"Now let's go home. I'm making a surprise dinner for Papa."

"Just for Papa?"

"No, for all of you. But Papa will not be able to enjoy it until later."

She and the children approached the tenement house. "I never get to see Papa any more." Nico's voice was sad. Discouraged.

"I'm sorry, son. This new job requires Papa to work long hours. He told me they received a huge order for garments that need to be placed in retail stores in time for Christmas shopping."

"Can I go to work with Papa?"

"I think there are laws in place here that frown on children working in factories. But that is beside the point. Papa wants you to go to school." She placed an arm around her son's shoulder. Her heart grieved for him. "Maybe we can get a new puppy for you soon."

Nico's face lit up. "When Mama?"

"I'll talk with Papa about it tonight."

Nico leaned his head on her arm. "Thank you, Mama."

Maria's heart warmed. She must introduce Nico to Enza Addevico's son Dominic as soon as possible.

* * * *

Luca returned home after eight o'clock that night. The children were already fast asleep when he arrived, and Maria was making a batch of homemade pasta. *"Ciao, Bella!"* He greeted her warmly as he entered their tiny flat.

Maria wiped her floured hands on her apron and embraced him. "Welcome home. You must be exhausted."

He sat down in the chair by the table where she was working. "It was a long day."

"Nearly twice the number of hours you used to work in Sicily."

Was she complaining or just stating a fact?

She went to the cupboard and retrieved a plate for his dinner. "How did things go?"

Luca raked his fingers through his hair and leaned his elbows on the table. "As good as can be expected, I guess."

"What do you mean 'I guess'?"

"Well, Mr. Dempsey is a tyrant of a boss. A taskmaster who continually makes sure we're meeting our quota for the day."

"That must be very stressful for you."

"It's just that I'm not used to having someone breathing down my neck all the time." He leaned back in his chair. "I don't want to do this for the rest of my life. One day, I'd really like to open my own tailor shop here in Brooklyn."

"That would be nice." She went to the stove where she'd warmed his dinner of fried eggplant and placed some on his plate. "If, that is, things work out for us here."

"I don't know why they shouldn't. We've been here only a few weeks. It's too soon to tell."

She placed the fried eggplant in front of him. "How are the people you work with? Friendly? Or do they keep to themselves?"

Should he tell her about Paulina? He didn't want to upset her any more than she already was. "There are four of us at my workstation. Jake Goldberg, a Jewish immigrant who is an amazing tailor. Then there's Gennaro Cappadona, a fellow Italian from Sicily. He sits to my left."

"And across from you?" The tone in her voice implied more than a simple question.

"Across from me is a Russian woman. Paulina Ivanov. Now, she's a problem."

Maria raised an eyebrow. "How so?"

Luca hesitated. "Well, I wasn't going to tell you this because I don't want to upset you, but she is a flirt. An annoying flirt. In fact, she so annoys me that I am planning to ask Mr. Dempsey to move me to another workstation."

"Do you think he will?"

"I'm not sure. I'm not on very good terms with him at the moment because of my refusal to work on Sundays. Jake said Mr. Dempsey doesn't particularly like Italians and Jews, so that's another strike against me. The most I can do is ask."

"And if he refuses?"

"If he refuses, I'm stuck working across from her. I have no other choice as far as I can see."

Maria wrinkled her forehead. "I will pray for you." Her gaze met his. "Just be careful, Luca."

Why did her words trouble him? Did she not trust him? "Of course, I will be careful."

"We should never think we are immune to any sin."

He placed a hand on hers. "That is wise counsel to follow."

She changed the subject. "Do you think we can get Nico the dog we promised him?"

Her question took Luca by surprise. "I think so. Did he bring up the topic?"

"No. But while coming home from buying vegetables, I saw him talking with some boys on the corner. They were smoking cigarettes and are not the kind of boys I want Nico befriending. I thought a dog would distract him."

Luca glanced over at his son, sound asleep on the upper bunk. "I think we can manage a dog. Maybe we can check the newspaper for someone who may be giving a dog away for free."

Maria placed her hand on Luca's. "Thank you. To be honest with you, I've been really concerned about Nico. I'm eager for him to meet Dominic, the twelve-year-old son of our neighbor Enza Addevico. They live just down the hall on our floor."

Luca's heart soared. Ever since insisting that Nico leave his dog behind, his relationship with his son had become strained. Not to mention that Luca was no longer spending time with him. When they worked together in the shop, they spent many hours together. But since their arrival in America, Luca hardly saw his son. "Yes. It would be good for Nico to have a friend his age. A good, decent boy who shares our values."

"There don't seem to be many decent boys around here. At least, not from what I have seen."

"I'm sure there are some. We just haven't found them yet." He finished the last bite of eggplant. "Thank you. It was delicious."

"I bought them from a vendor on our street. He is a *paesano* and gave me a discount."

She removed his plate from the table and walked toward the sink. "By the way, you got a letter today from the American Bible Society."

Luca's heart stirred. "Interesting. Must be a reply regarding my inquiry. I'll read it before we go to bed."

He rose and, taking her gently by the shoulders, turned her toward him. "Maria, are you happy?"

"I'm fine, Luca." Her averted eyes belied her words.

He gently pulled her toward him. "Tell me the truth. I must know."

Her gaze met his. "Luca, this move has been extremely difficult for me. Leaving beautiful *Bella Terra* behind for a tiny flat in a noisy city hit me hard. Most of all, leaving Mama and my sisters behind has shaken me to the core. I still haven't heard from Mama or Cristina. I still don't know if Mama is all right. But I am a fighter. I will do my best to adapt to our new life. If God told us to come here, then He has good things in store for us here. I will trust Him." She caressed his cheek. "And I will trust you."

"You have no idea what that means to me."

She smiled a smile that did not come from her heart.

And he returned a smile that did not come from his.

Chapter Thirteen

Maria was already sound asleep by the time Luca got around to reading the letter from the American Bible Society. He eagerly tore open the seal, unfolded the letter, and placed it on the kitchen table.

The sounds of chattering voices, mingled with the putrid stench of days-old garbage, filtered up from the street below through the partially open door that led to the balcony. Through the paper-thin walls, Luca could hear the young couple next door arguing over money, while on the other side of his flat, a neighbor played an accordion.

Memories of *Bella Terra* flooded Luca's mind. He missed Sicily. The old homestead. The hills. The silence of the night broken only by the soft chirping of cicadas.

As for natural beauty, Brooklyn was a far cry from his native land. But natural beauty didn't put food on the table.

Luca jerked his thoughts back to the present. One of Satan's chief devices was to get God's children to dwell on the past. It was a trap many fell into, to their great detriment. Luca would not be one of them.

Seated with his Italian-English dictionary at his side, he interpreted each word of the letter into Italian, one by one, carefully printing the translation on a sheet of paper. His eyes were heavy with sleep, especially in the dim light of the small lamp he'd placed on the table, but he could not rest until he knew what the letter said.

As he read each English word and compared it with the Italian word, he noticed patterns emerging that he could use in learning English. Although he wanted to learn the language of his new homeland quickly, Will Dempsey's insistence on his doing so had put Luca under additional pressure. Giulio had been most gracious to serve as his interpreter, but Luca could not always rely on Giulio to help him. His friend had his own job to do and his own matters to take care of.

Luca painstakingly copied each translation from the dictionary on to his sheet of paper. When he had finished translating each word, he read his finished work:

Dear Mr. Tonetta:

Greetings in the precious Name of Jesus!

We were delighted to hear from you and welcome you to America! We trust that you are adapting well and settling into your new life here.

You inquired about Jonathan Mitchell, the missionary who led you to Christ many years ago. Currently, he is stationed in Japan but will be returning to the States in about six months. We forwarded your letter to him. We know he will be very happy to hear from you. You should be hearing from him soon.

We want to let you know that we would be honored to have you work with the American Bible Society as a volunteer lay missionary. In fact, we have a mission outreach in your area, in Brooklyn, and would like you to consider working with us there in your spare time. The need is great, but the laborers are few.

We look forward to hearing from you and pray God's blessings upon you and your family.

Sincerely in Christ,

Ryce Emerson, President

Luca carefully folded the letter, his heart stirring at the prospect of working at the Brooklyn Mission. His dream of preaching the Gospel in America was now within reach. God had opened a door, and Luca must walk through it. How wonderful it would be to share the love of Christ with the hurting, the homeless, and the lost! How wonderful to bring healing to his very neighborhood and, by extension, to his new homeland!

Despite its established position in the world as the best nation on earth, America still had its problems, as he was discovering day by day. The Industrial Revolution had spawned a host of challenges with its growing number of factories, abuse of child labor laws, and political corruption. Not to mention the many social issues that had resulted from the mass immigration that was taking place. His very tenement house was a prime example. Although many good people lived there, many who cared nothing about morality or the law lived there as well.

Yes, Luca wanted very much to volunteer at the Brooklyn Mission. The only problem was making the time. With a work schedule of eighty-four hours a week, he had no time to breathe let alone volunteer at the Brooklyn Mission. He hardly saw Maria and the children as it was.

Luca's heart sank. His job was interfering with his destiny. Yet, he needed his job to support his family. If only the job at the mission were a paying job.

Of course, after the Christmas season, his work schedule would drop to sixty hours per week. Or, at least, he hoped so. That would leave him Saturdays to volunteer a few hours.

He placed the letter in the top drawer of his dresser and knelt by the side of his bed, bowing his head in prayer. "Father, if working at the Brooklyn Mission is Your will for me, You will have to make a way."

I am the Way.

With the Lord's comforting words reverberating in his heart, Luca climbed into bed. Maria's soft, steady breathing beside him calmed his soul. How he loved this woman of his heart! How he wanted to give her a wonderful life!

He lay on his back, arms under his head, and stared at the ceiling. The dream of opening his own shop stirred his soul yet again. Owning his own business would enable him to set his own hours and would allow him time to volunteer at the Mission and to preach the Gospel.

The more he pondered the thought, the more he liked it. But he would have to save a good deal of money before he'd be in a position to start his own business.

A thought suddenly came to him. Maybe, in the meantime, Maria would like to volunteer at the Mission a few hours a week. It would help her to learn English while ministering to others for the cause of Christ. It would provide her with good brothers and sisters in the Lord who shared her values.

It would ground her in a ministry both she and Luca could share together once he opened his own shop.

And it would give her a sense of purpose that she desperately needed to adapt well in their new country.

Luca's chest lightened at the prospect of preaching the Gospel with his precious wife. Perhaps this was the ultimate reason God had brought them to America. To make their marriage a witness of Christ's love for the Church and the Church's love for Him as they worked side by side in ministry.

Luca whispered the meditation of his heart. "Not my will, Father, but Yours be done."

Yes, My son. You have chosen well.

With the Lord's comforting words reverberating in his heart, Luca fell fast asleep.

* * * *

The knock on the door startled Maria from her mending. She put down the old pair of socks and told Valeria and Anna to remain still in front of the open balcony door.

"Coming!" She called through her apartment door. It was the latest word she'd learned in her quest to master the English language.

She opened the door and found the postman waiting there, his mail-laden, leather bag hanging from his shoulder.

"Good morning. This letter is for Maria Tonetta."

Maria's stomach tensed. This could be none other than a letter from her family in Sicily. She pointed to herself and spoke in broken English. "I am Maria Tonetta."

The postman smiled. "Then this is for you."

Although she did not understand his words, she understood his gesture as he handed her the letter. With trembling hand, she took it from him, thanked him, and closed the door.

Her heart pounded as she sat down in the chair next to the kitchen table and opened the letter. What did it say? Had Mama died?

Should she wait for Luca to come home before reading it?

No. She could not wait. She had to know what had happened to Mama the day she'd fainted as their ship pulled out of port. The image of Mama collapsing into Cristina's arms had tormented Maria's mind ever since.

"Mama, will you play with us?" Valeria's voice burst into her consciousness.

"In a moment, sweet one. Mama has something very important to do right now."

"What's more important than playing?"

"I'll play with you in a few moments, darling. I promise."

"Okay, Mama."

Maria gazed at the handwriting on the envelope. It was her sister Cristina's. That meant Mama had not been well enough to write it herself. Her hands shaking, Maria tore off the seal and unfolded the letter. The crinkled onionskin paper shook as she began to read.

My dearest sister Maria,

This is Cristina writing to you. You must have been eagerly awaiting my response to your letter. I want to assure you that Mama is well. After your departure, we took her to a hospital in Palermo. It was determined she collapsed because of emotional distress. She was treated and released. We spent the night in a hotel in Palermo and departed the next morning to return to Ribera. From there, Salvatore took us by wagon back to Bella Terra.

Maria breathed a long sigh of relief, despite her remorse at having caused Mama such distress. "Thank You, Lord! Thank You for watching over Mama."

She continued reading.

We all miss you very much. Mama still cries when she speaks of you. She especially misses Nico, Valeria, and Anna. They were her pride and joy, you know.

Was Cristina trying to make her feel guilty? She didn't have to try too hard.

I find myself weeping too, along with Mama. How we wish you had remained in Sicily!

We have heard from Don Franco. He is doing well, although he misses Bella Terra very much. Things on the farm are not doing well. Several of the hired hands have left for better opportunities. I can't blame them. We still have Salvatore and a handful of the old-timers. But they are getting old, and it is becoming increasingly difficult for them to work. Pietro, Luciana, Mama, and I are wondering if we should consider selling the farm and moving to an apartment in Pisano. But I sincerely hope it won't come to that. I couldn't bear to leave Bella Terra. Frankly, I don't know how you did it, dear sister of mine.

Maria's heart clenched. She had asked herself the same question many times.

How about you, Maria? How are you faring? And Luca and the children? We hear stories of life in America— some good, some not so good. But I can understand why many have left. Sicily is growing poorer and poorer by the day. At times, we wonder if we ourselves should leave. But Mama is too old and too frail. I could never subject her to the ordeal of moving to a foreign country at her age. In fact, just the thought of a possible move to the village overwhelms her. She insists she will die at Bella Terra.

I look forward to hearing about your life in America. Does Luca like his job? What does Brooklyn look like? I have heard there is a huge bridge there. Have you seen it?

Maria smiled at her sister's multiple questions. Cristina had always been the talkative one among the three daughters. Papa would often remind her that when the mouth is shut, the mind is open. But his words didn't seem to have taken root despite Cristina's sincere efforts.

Tears filled Maria's eyes at the memory of her precious sister. Would she ever see her again? Would she ever see her other sister, Luciana, again?

Would she ever see Mama again?

Well, dear sister, that is all the news for now. I hope you are happy in your new land. I send you, Luca, and the children a big hug and much love. Please write soon!

Your devoted sister,

Cristina

With tears streaming down her face, Maria folded the letter and held it close to her heart.

Valeria approached her. "Mama, why are you crying?"

Maria gathered her elder daughter into her arms. "Mama's fine, dear one. Don't worry."

"But you used to laugh all the time, Mama. I don't like it when you cry."

Maria brushed aside a wisp of curly hair from her daughter's forehead. "I don't like it, either."

"Then why do you cry?"

Maria hugged her daughter tightly. "Sometimes the tears come without our wanting them."

Valeria buried her face in Maria's chest. "Will you play with us now, Mama?"

Maria swallowed hard. "Yes, darling. Mama will play with you."

Tonight, after the children were asleep, Maria would write a long letter to Cristina, detailing their life in America. The details would make Cristina happy.

And, perhaps, provide some relief for the deep ache in Maria's soul.

* * * *

Luca awakened at the crack of dawn. A sliver of sunlight filtered through the thick beige curtains Maria had placed over the balcony door, casting soft shadows over their tiny, one-room flat. She'd sewn them herself in a meager attempt to give them some much-needed privacy and to add a touch of beauty to their humble abode.

An attempt Luca appreciated with all of his heart.

Day by day, she seemed to be adapting to her new surroundings. In a few short months, he'd have his old Maria back. At least, he hoped so.

He washed and dressed for work. Then he sat at the

kitchen table for his early morning coffee with his beloved. The children were still asleep and would not awaken for another hour. He missed hugging them before leaving for work. Now, with his longer work hours, he rarely saw them at night, either. Not a good thing. But, for the time being, he had no other choice. He'd be sure to spend a lot of time with them on Sundays.

The smell of espresso filled the tiny flat. Dressed in a white cotton bathrobe, Maria stood at the stove, pouring two cups of the dark, rich brew for her and Luca. She brought them to the kitchen table and placed Luca's cup in front of him. She sat down beside him. "I received a letter from Cristina."

Luca's heart leapt. "Praise the Lord! What did she say?"

"Mama is alive! Thank God! That's the most important thing."

"Thank God, indeed! You must feel so relieved."

"You can't imagine what a load has lifted from my heart. I didn't realize how worried I've been all these weeks."

"What happened? Is Mama all right?"

"She fainted at the dock as our ship was pulling out. Watching her daughter and grandchildren leave and not knowing if she would ever see them again must have been wrenching for her."

A twinge of guilt niggled at Luca's soul.

"It turned out that she was overcome with emotion at our leaving. Luciana, Cristina, and Pietro took her to a hospital in Palermo where she was treated and then discharged. They stayed in Palermo overnight and returned home the next day. She has recovered and, so far, is doing well."

Luca's heart clenched as another twinge of guilt assailed him. "Maria, do you hold our move to America against me?"

She remained silent for a moment, contemplating her response. "Luca, when I married you, I promised to follow you wherever God led. I have kept my promise. To say it has been easy would be a lie. But to say that I hold anything against you would also be a lie."

He caressed her hand. "Each day I am more and more convinced that we are in the center of God's will."

She grew pensive. "That is the only safe place to be."

How thankful Luca was for such a godly wife!

"Now, I must show you something before I leave for work." Luca went to his dresser and retrieved the translation he had done the night before of the letter from the American Bible Society. He handed it to Maria.

She read the translation and then looked up at him. "You did this yourself?"

"Yes."

She smiled. "I am impressed."

Luca's heart warmed. "Well, what do you think?"

"I think working at the Brooklyn Mission would be wonderful, but how can you take advantage of the opportunity with the long hours you work? You certainly cannot take any more time away from your family. The children see you only on Sundays as it is."

"I agree." He took the letter from her hands and placed it on the kitchen table. Then, he took both her hands in his. "As I was lying awake last night, I had an idea. I thought you might like to volunteer at the Mission until I am free to open my own tailoring business. At that point, I would be able to join you in ministry in the evenings and on Saturdays."

"But, Luca, it might be a very long time before you can start your own business. You know how expensive equipment is. Plus, you'd have to have enough money to rent space somewhere." She lowered her eyes. "As for my volunteering there, that sounds like a good idea. I think I would like that very much."

"What you said about starting my own business is true, dear one. But we can do it. In fact, I will start inquiring now into good locations for a shop and into the costs. I'll talk to other tailors who have their own shops. Jake Goldberg might know of someone willing to advise me."

"Speaking of Jake Goldberg, how are things with Paulina?"

"Why do you ask?"

She smiled demurely. "Because I'm a woman."

He chuckled and then turned serious. "Are you worried?"

Her gaze was steady and serene as she took his hands. "Luca, I trust you implicitly. I also know Satan's devices and how they can deceive the human heart. We must live in the constant knowledge that any one of us could commit any sin."

The sobriety of her words struck him with force. "You are right. I promise you I will be very careful. Today I will ask Mr. Dempsey to relocate me to another station."

"And if he doesn't?"

"Then I will tell Paulina about Jesus."

"Don't you think you should do that anyway? Regardless of where your workstation is located? It seems obvious she is not one of His followers."

"I will follow Holy Spirit's leading. Meanwhile, pray for me."

"I do, Luca. Every day."

"Thank you, darling." He kissed her soundly. "Well, it's time for me to go to work. I will see you late tonight. I pray you have a good day, sweetheart."

"I pray the same for you, my precious Luca."

Chapter Fourteen

Luca arrived at the workshop a few minutes before his six o'clock a.m. starting time. Will had told the employees that when they finished their quota for the day, they could leave. Luca wanted to get a head start on his bundles so he could leave earlier that evening and meet Maria and the children at the Mission. Maria had decided to volunteer and now looked forward to ministering there several times a week.

A bright autumn sun filled the workshop. The custodian had opened several of the windows, letting in the brisk November air. Luca took in a deep breath of it and filled his lungs. Sounds of life from the street below floated upward, inspiring the renewed hope that a new day brought.

After pouring himself a cup of coffee from the coffeepot, Luca went directly to his workstation. To his surprise, Paulina was already busy working. Strange, since on most mornings, she arrived late.

He looked around the room. So far, no one else had arrived. His muscles tensed, and his spirit went on high alert.

"Good morning, Luca." She smiled seductively and batted her long, dark eyelashes as she spoke.

"Good morning." He sat down at his workstation and took the cover off his sewing machine. It didn't help matters that she sat directly across from him. As much as he tried to avoid her gaze, her very location made it difficult to do so. Not to mention the fact that her eyes held wrong intentions.

He prayed silently for wisdom. Paulina needed Jesus, and he would trust God for an opportunity to share the Gospel with her.

The delivery boy had already placed the pile of garment pieces on the bench next to the workstation. The size of the pile threatened to dishearten Luca, but he attuned his mind to God's grace working in him to get the job done. Just as he lived one day at a time, so would he work one garment piece at a time.

Paulina's lilting voice echoed in the large, empty room. "Looks as though we're the only two early birds this morning."

He did not miss the insinuation. "The delivery boy must be the third early bird, since our garment pieces are already here. One day I will meet him, I hope." Perhaps, if she knew they were not alone, she'd keep to herself.

"Yes, but he's gone. You'd have to arrive around four o'clock a.m. to catch him. He delivers batches of garments to several other factories in Brooklyn as well. Our factory is the first one on his list." She smiled again. "So, as I said, we are alone." Her last words held a tinge of sultriness.

In his spirit, he heard the serpent's hiss, but Luca remained undaunted by her comment. "Jake and Gennaro will soon be here, as will the others. It is very close to starting time." He could hardly wait until another worker arrived.

Paulina took a sip of her coffee. Her almond-shaped dark eyes, skirting the rim of the cup, pierced him like hot, black coals.

She put down her cup. "Has anyone ever told you how handsome you are?"

Luca wanted to run. "Yes, my wife."

"Ah, so you agree that you are handsome." She hesitated. "Very handsome."

"Thank you. Now I think it's time we get to work."

She ignored his words. "Do you think I am beautiful?"

Luca shifted in his chair. "Paulina, this is not appropriate conversation for the workplace."

"But it is for another place."

Bile rose to his throat. The woman was outright brazen. "You are wrong. This is not appropriate conversation for any place. Have you no fear of God? Now, if you please, I want to get started on my day's quota."

"We can talk while we work." She would not give up.

"I find it difficult to carry on a conversation while I am working."

"But you would if you could?"

Luca felt like Joseph with Potiphar's wife. "Paulina, let's get one thing straight, right off the bat. I am here to work, not to talk. More importantly, I am a happily married man with a wonderful wife and three beautiful children. Whatever your motives, you will get nowhere with me. Do you understand?"

Her face hardened. "Very well. You have made your point clear."

"Good. Now let's get to work."

She rose, deliberately leaning forward enough to reveal what should be kept hidden. "I'm going to get myself another cup of coffee. May I refill your coffee cup?"

He really could have used a second cup of coffee, but to accept her offer would not be wise. "No, thank you. I'll get myself another cup later."

She gave him a questioning look. "Suit yourself." She sauntered toward the coffee pot and returned a few moments later. "I'm from Moscow. What about you?"

Was he being rude in not answering her question? "I'm from Pisano. A tiny village on the southwestern coast of Sicily."

"I know Sicily. I visited there with my late mother several years ago. One of her best friends lived in Messina."

Luca couldn't ignore her mention of her loss. "I'm sorry about the loss of your mother."

"Thank you. She was all I had left in the world. When

177

she died, I decided I needed a change and came to America."

Luca tried to talk over the whirring of his sewing machine. "How long have you been here?"

"Two years." She hesitated. "Two lonely years."

Her emphasis on the word *lonely* did not escape him.

"I will pray that God fills your loneliness."

She gave him a seductive smile. "He could fill it through you."

The woman had no shame. None whatsoever. She treated sin lightly, as though it were nothing.

Luca sighed. He rose to stretch his legs and walked over to the window.

She followed him.

His muscles tensed as Paulina drew up to his side. Too close to his side. He moved a few paces away.

"The day is beautiful, is it not?" She drew closer to him again, giving him a sultry smile. The fragrance of her perfume brushed against his nostrils. "The night time will be even more beautiful if we spend it together." Her words were barely a whisper.

Heat rose to Luca's face. He turned toward her. "Paulina, do you not realize that what you are doing is sin? Blatant sin?"

She lifted her chin. "Love is never sin."

"What you are suggesting is not love. It is adultery and fornication. Plain and simple. Have you no fear of the Lord? No sense of guilt? No conscience?"

"I got rid of my conscience a long time ago."

Did he detect a hint of remorse in her voice?

Her jaw squared, and her eyes narrowed into slits. "You are a hard man to break, Luca Tonetta. You have no idea what you are missing by resisting me." With that, she stalked away from the window and returned to her workstation.

Luca whispered a prayer for wisdom to His Heavenly Father.

Remember, My son, that you are not wrestling against flesh and blood, but against principalities and powers, against the rulers of darkness of this world, against spiritual wickedness in high places.

The Father's words comforted him. This was not a battle to be waged in the natural world, but in the supernatural. A battle he would win only with much prayer. "Lord, give me strength and wisdom. Protect me from all evil." Luca sighed. "And please help Paulina to see the truth."

Luca returned to his workstation.

Paulina ignored him.

Part of Luca was thankful, but another part of him worried for her soul. Paulina was lost in sin and needed Jesus. Perhaps the Lord had placed him at her workstation to lead her to Christ. Did not Jesus dine with prostitutes and other sinners?

Finally, she spoke. "I thought you were a tailor, not a preacher." She clipped her words.

Luca chuckled. "I'm both." He recognized his opportunity. "What do you think about Jesus?"

"I don't think about Him."

"Why not?"

"Why should I? He's never done anything for me. So I leave Him alone, and He leaves me alone."

"But He doesn't leave you alone."

"What do you mean?"

"This conversation we are having now—about Jesus—was ordained by Him."

She gave Luca a look as though he'd lost his mind. "I think you were right about getting to work." With that, she took another sleeve from the garment pile and began to sew.

Luca was relieved but disappointed that he could not continue the conversation about Jesus. But not talking at all was better than small talk. He had no time for small talk.

Truth be told, what he really had no time for was temptation. But since when did the devil oblige? Throughout the day, Paulina enticed him with her eyes, her demure smile, her occasional bits of conversation. By the end of the day, Luca was more exhausted from the strain of being the target of temptation than from the physical labor of attaching sleeves to more than one hundred jackets.

How long would he be able to endure this situation? At the next opportunity, he would ask Will to move him to another workstation.

But something inside Luca told him to wait.

Is that You, Lord, or is it the enemy?

****

Will sat across from Paulina in the quaint, little Italian seafood restaurant where they'd gone to have dinner. Located in Queens, the restaurant was far enough away not to arouse suspicion of their relationship nor gossip that would jeopardize his job. No one knew him in Queens. At least, no one he knew. As for Paulina, her friends never ventured far from her neighborhood in Brooklyn. Chances were good she'd be undetected here.

Despite the precautions, Will's gaze darted around the restaurant. Guilt had a way of embedding itself into one's conscience, like a leech embedding itself into one's skin. It had to be pulled out gently and in such a way as not to harm or leave residual damage in the surrounding area.

The restaurant bustled with the chatter of people, young, old, and in-between. Children squirmed, cranky at being out past their bedtime. Young couples stared into each other's eyes, forgetting the food in front of them. Elderly couples stared at the food in front of them, forgetting the spouse that sat across from them.

The aroma of fried cod and garlic filled the air, whetting

Will's appetite. He needed some food in his belly. After this morning's hangover, he hadn't eaten a thing all day.

A waiter approached their table and took their order. "Your appetizers will be here shortly. Would you like some wine?"

Will hesitated, but only briefly. "Yes. Bring a bottle of your best Chianti."

The waiter smiled and nodded. "Right away, sir."

Will shouldn't have ordered the wine. He rationalized he'd done it for Paulina. Truth was he couldn't resist the urge.

He also couldn't resist the urge to possess this woman in front of him. What had become of him? An alcoholic he was, but a fornicator? At one time, that had been out of his league. Before he married Katie, he'd never known another woman. And while he was married to Katie, he'd been faithful to her.

Mama's words rang in his ears. *"One sin makes the next one easier, son. So stay away from all sin."*

His soul cringed. What would Mama think if she saw him now? Just the thought made him blush.

He took Paulina's hand. They'd been seeing each other for almost seven months now. She'd agreed to celebrate the occasion with dinner.

And dessert.

He rubbed her fingers. "Happy Anniversary. Seven months already. Can you believe it?"

"I can believe it." A sad look crossed her face.

Will's muscles tensed. Something wasn't right between them, but he couldn't quite put his finger on it. "Aren't you happy about it?"

She lowered her gaze and then lifted it again. "The longer we're together, the less I feel you really love me."

"What do you mean?"

"I mean I feel you are using me."

He stiffened. "Well, if you feel that way, why are you agreeing to it?"

Her eyes widened with fire. "So, now you are blaming me?"

"Look, Paulina, it takes two to waltz. If you don't want to waltz, just let me know."

"It's not that I don't want to waltz. It's that …." She floundered in her attempt to back-pedal.

"It's what?"

"It's that I'm developing other interests."

An alarm went on in Will's heart. She was talking about Luca Tonetta. He pressed her. "What kind of other interests?"

She withdrew her hand from his and brushed back a stray wisp of hair from her cheek. "Let's not talk about it, Will."

"Fine." He knew better than to insist. He'd try another angle to get the info he was looking for. "So, how do you like working with Luca Tonetta?"

Guilt glazed her eyes as she drew in a deep breath and smiled. "I like him." She folded her hands on the table. "I like him a lot."

Will's stomach tied itself into a tight knot. He'd gotten his answer. Paulina's "other interests" focused on Luca Tonetta. But Will couldn't let on. Instead, he played along with her. "As much as I hate to admit it, Luca is one of the nicest Italians I've met. In fact, if all Italians were like him, things would be a lot better at the shop."

She eyed him with contempt. "What do you mean? Italians are decent people. Hard-working. Kind-hearted. And—I might add—fun."

Maybe Will could still hold on to her heart. "Speaking of fun, how would you like to have some tonight?"

Her facial expression fell. "I'm sorry, Will. I'm really

tired tonight." She gave him a sidelong glance. "It's all of those long hours you're making us work."

He squared his jaw. "I'm not making you work those long hours. Oliver Cramdon is."

"Well, whether it's you or Oliver Cramdon, the fact is we're the ones working the long hours."

Paulina hesitated, her eyes averting him. "Will, I think I should let you know now—sooner than later—that I don't want to continue in this relationship."

A boulder struck his chest, knocking the wind out of him. "What do you mean? We've been moving right along, with no problems." Bile rose to his throat. "None, that is, until that Tonetta guy started working for me." The words spilled from his lips. Why hadn't he kept his mouth shut?

She lowered her eyes and remained silent.

He leaned back in his chair and folded his arms. "You know he's married, don't you? Married with three kids?"

She raised her gaze and smiled slyly. "That's never stopped me before."

To Will's surprise, a righteous anger welled up within him. *Where did that come from? Must be a residual from Mama's teachings.*

He threw his napkin down on the table. "You really are a tramp, aren't you?"

"And so are you, Will Dempsey!" She shouted the words, attracting the attention of the entire restaurant.

Heat rose to his face. "Great! Now everybody knows we're here."

"So what?" She stood, grabbing her purse. "Goodbye, Will. I've had enough of this charade."

"Are you leaving your job, too?"

She raised both eyebrows. "I hadn't thought of that. Are you firing me?"

More than anything, he wanted to say "Yes." But something held him in check. Maybe he really was beginning to feel something genuine for Paulina Ivanov. "No. I won't fire you. That would be cruel. But I will change your workstation. I don't want a good man like Luca to be corrupted by a loose woman like you."

A strange look crossed her face. "Will Dempsey, you are a far better man than you think you are."

Surprising words coming from Paulina. Maybe there was some decency left in her as well.

Chapter Fifteen

Paulina paced her flat, wringing her hands. She seethed at Luca's rejection. Never before had a man responded in such a way to her advances. Was she losing her touch?

Luca's rejection only made her more determined to subjugate him. To bring him low.

To take him down completely.

Who did he think he was? Some superhuman being? Some angel?

Some saint immune to sin?

She scoffed.

No matter that Luca loved his God, his wife, and his children. He was still a man. A human of flesh and bones.

And she was still a woman.

Any man worthy of his manhood would not be able to resist the wiles of a woman who offered herself to him.

Especially a woman like her.

She squared her jaw and formulated the evil plan in her mind. Luca Tonetta would pay—and pay well—for insulting her.

And no one but she would be any the wiser as to the real culprit in the crime.

She walked to the large window overlooking the street below. Night had fallen, and gaslights illuminated the busy street. From the sixth floor, pedestrians looked like insects and buggies like toys. A light rain fell, splashing droplets of water against the windowpane of her balcony door.

She drew in a deep breath as her plan came into focus. In one of his weaker moments, Will had been foolish enough to tell her where he kept the moneybox containing the week's profits. Tomorrow morning, before the workshop opened, she would steal the money and hide it at Luca's workstation, in his bundle of garment pieces. When Will discovered the theft, she'd point the finger of guilt at Luca Tonetta. She would tell Will that Luca had been complaining of not having enough money to make ends meet.

A search would prove her accusation true.

Paulina smiled. That would show Luca Tonetta how much his purity paid off. How far his self-righteousness would get him.

How much his love for his God really mattered.

Several years behind bars would teach him how wrong he'd been in refusing her advances.

The more she pondered the idea, the more she liked it. Tomorrow morning, while Tony delivered the garment bundles at each workstation, she would slip into Will's office and execute her plan.

* * * *

Will Dempsey was no fool. During the past several weeks, Paulina had grown cold toward him and hot toward Luca Tonetta. It didn't take a genius to notice it. All Will had to do was look into Paulina's eyes when she was around Luca, and the knot in Will's belly would tighten.

Why did it even matter to him? She was nothing more than a temporary fling to fill his time.

Or was she?

Had he begun to grow fond of her in a way that surpassed mere lust?

The fact she didn't love him hadn't mattered until now. He'd been content to go along with the charade, pretending that maybe one day she'd come around and develop some real feelings for him. That maybe one day he'd rediscover something—or someone—to live for.

But now she'd dumped him and poised her wicked claws over Luca Tonetta. A good man, despite the fact he was Italian. Should Will warn him? Or would his warning be misconstrued as the raging jealousy it also was?

To Luca's credit, he'd resisted Paulina's advances. She'd had the nerve to mention as much to Will. Nothing like twisting the knife in his heart. But Luca's rejection of her advances was not surprising, given he'd also demonstrated his good character by refusing to work on the Sabbath. Yet, Luca's rejection had only fueled her determination to make him fall from grace. She wouldn't be happy until he succumbed to her wiles.

Will sighed. Truth be told, part of him wanted to see Luca fall from grace as well. It would be a fitting vengeance that would satisfy his hatred of Italians. But another part of him wanted to protect Luca from a woman whom Will knew firsthand could bring him to destruction.

Will wiped his palm across his face and stared at the Brooklyn Bridge. Thick, heavy fog covered its towers, obscuring them from view. Much like the fog that clouded his mind, keeping him from knowing what to do.

"God, what should I do?" The prayer rose, unbidden, from Will's heart, surprising him. Maybe there was some decency left in him after all.

He leaned back in his chair. He'd talk to Luca later about Paulina. No sense taking a chance Luca might be naïve, miss one of her tricks, and fall into Paulina's trap.

But for now, Will needed to tally the wholesale profits for the week and send them to Oliver Cramdon. The number of wholesale vendors buying directly from Will's workshop had doubled over the last six months. Cramdon's decision to sell directly to wholesalers had produced better results than expected, but it had also added to Will's job the responsibility of collecting payment for the orders. Every Friday, an armored guard from Cramdon's office came to pick up the week's profits.

As if Will didn't have enough headaches.

After he made sure his office door was locked, Will went to his desk to retrieve the moneybox that he kept in the bottom drawer.

This past week had been a good one. Christmas sales were already increasing, and Will's workshop was at the forefront in productivity. And he wanted to keep it that way. Cramdon had this little contest going each year among his workshops. The one with the highest profit got a generous bonus at the start of the new year to divide among the employees. For five straight years, Will's shop had been the winner. He wasn't about to lose his lead now.

He opened the bottom drawer and reached toward the back of it.

But the moneybox was gone!

* * * *

Maria's stomach tightened as her mind drifted to Luca. He'd been distant lately. More quiet than usual. Truth be told, his mention of Paulina's annoying flirtations bothered Maria more than she was willing to admit. Not that she didn't trust Luca. She didn't trust women. Their wiles were no match for a man. Even a Godly man like Luca. A wicked woman could bring a man down without his ever realizing what was happening to him. During her growing-up years back in Sicily, she'd overheard countless stories of good men being brought low and whole families ruined as a result by conniving women.

As Maria kneaded the dough for the evening meal, she vented her frustrations upon the innocent lump. Back and forth, back and forth, she dug the heel of her palm into the pliable dough, kneading it until it was ready to be formed into a loaf. She then molded it into shape with both of her hands and laid it in the loaf pan. From there, she put it in the oven for baking.

Luca had promised to be home early tonight so he could join her and the children at the Brooklyn Mission after dinner. The ministry had become a focal point of her life, and she couldn't wait until Luca could devote more time to it as well.

"Valeria, please set the table. And add a place for Papa. He will be eating with us tonight."

"Yes, Mama. I almost forget what Papa looks like."

An arrow pierced Maria's heart. No wonder. Luca left before the children awakened and returned after they were asleep. "Well, tonight you will be able to get a good look at him, all right?"

"Yes, Mama. I will make sure to look at Papa long and hard."

Should Maria laugh or cry at Valeria's comment?

Anna mimicked her sister. "Mama, I will make sure to look at Papa long and hard, too."

Valeria shouted at her sister. "Why do you always want to say what I say and do what I do?"

Maria wiped her floured hands on the towel around her waist. "Valeria, do you not know that Anna's desire to imitate you grows out of her love and admiration for you?"

A perplexed look crossed Valeria's face.

"Yes. Anna loves you so much she wants to be and act just like you." Maria took Valeria's little hands in hers. "In the same way, Jesus is pleased when we desire to imitate Him."

Nico crossed the room from his place by the balcony door. "Mama, it's snowing. Will we be going to the Mission tonight?"

"All the more reason to go, my son. The bad weather will bring many more of the homeless in for shelter, and the staff will be in much need of our help."

"Now, please wash your hands for dinner. Papa will be home soon."

But thirty minutes later, there was still no sign of Luca.

Chapter Sixteen

The wall clock showed only a few more minutes to closing time. Luca reached down into his garment bin for another sleeve. Only two more to sew.

Outside, darkness had settled over the city. As winter approached, the days grew shorter and shorter. Soon Christmas would be upon them.

A sudden ruckus at the main door disrupted Luca's thoughts. He looked up from his sewing as Will Dempsey stormed into the workstation, his eyes aflame. Behind him were two police officers.

Will shouted above the din, raising his hand in the air. "Attention! Attention! I want everyone's attention now."

Sewing machines stopped whirring. Chatter ceased.

All eyes turned toward Will.

"A large sum of money has been stolen from the workshop. These two police officers are here to conduct a search. Please remain silent as you cooperate."

One officer went to the far end of the workshop to begin his search. The other began with the table next to Luca's.

Luca glanced at Paulina. The smug look on her face did not portend well for the occasion. She gazed at him with a triumphant look in her eye.

The officer searched every nook and cranny of the workstation. Drawers. Storage bins. Garment bundles. Piles of finished garments. He even required each person to stand so he could examine his or her chair.

Satisfied that the first table had cleared inspection, the officer came to Luca's table. He searched Luca's drawers.

Nothing. He searched Luca's basket of supplies. Nothing there, either. When he came to Luca's bin containing the remaining garments to be sewn, he reached deep down into the bin and retrieved the moneybox. He straightened and glared at Luca. "I think we've found our thief."

All eyes turned toward Luca.

Luca froze. "What do you mean?"

"You know right well what I mean, Mr.—?"

"Tonetta. Luca Tonetta."

The officer turned toward Will. "Looks like we've got your man."

Luca stood. "But I do not understand what you mean!"

The officer first grabbed one of his wrists and then the other. "I mean you're under arrest."

"But this is impossible."

"Yeah, yeah." The officer placed the iron handcuffs around Luca's wrists. "They all say the same thing—'Who, me?'" He snapped the handcuffs shut. "Look, buddy. I may have been born at night, but I wasn't born last night."

At the sound of the ominous click, something died inside Luca. The click of the handcuffs around his wrists was like a bullet through his heart. To be so humiliated, and in front of his co-workers, was more than he could bear. Anger welled up within him. He was innocent. Someone had planted that money in his garment pile. Someone with a desire for vengeance against him.

Someone with the desire to see him destroyed.

There was only one person in the whole world who could have done this.

Paulina Ivanov.

One look at her triumphant eyes as he was being dragged away told Luca he was right.

* * * *

The Raymond Street County Jail in Brooklyn, sometimes called Brooklyn's Bastille, was a literal Hell on Earth. Situated at the corner of Raymond and Willoughby Streets, at the edge of Fort Greene Park and not far from Luca's tenement house, the prison wasn't fit for animals, let alone humans. Its reputation as a dungeon of despair, despised even by devils, reached far and wide.

Luca shivered in the cold confines of his tiny, pitch-black cell. The unbearable stench rising from the filthy planks of the thick, oak-timbered floors burned his nostrils. The only light came from a flickering candle in the cell of a more fortunate prisoner across the narrow hallway who'd paid for the privilege of candlelight.

With no opportunity to contact Maria, Luca had been brought here straight from the workshop on charges of theft. He would be held in custody until a trial would prove him either guilty or innocent.

Sitting on the wooden slab that served both as a bench and a bed, he buried his face in his hands. Hot tears slid down his cheeks. In only a few moments, his American dream had turned into a nightmare of the worst proportions.

Would he ever awaken from it?

His mind raced through the events of the last several days, looking for some clue to his great misfortune. How had he ended up here? What had he done to deserve such a punishment?

Did Paulina hate him so much she would destroy his life? This was her doing. He was sure of it. The look in her eyes had told him as much as he was being led away by the police. She'd taken vengeance on him because of his refusal to acquiesce to her sexual advances.

Plain and simple.

He swallowed hard.

This was what Joseph must have felt like when he was

imprisoned as a result of the false accusations of Potiphar's wife. Yet, Paulina had not accused Luca of sexual assault. She'd implicated him in a crime that would not involve her word against his. A crime that would be in the public view, supporting her innocence and Luca's guilt.

He fell to his knees beside the bench. "Father, You are sovereign. You knew before all time that I would be placed in this prison. Before You, I am innocent of all crime. That is my peace, Father. A clean conscience. Please help me. Please expose the truth. Please watch over Maria and the children while I am here. Please get me out of here quickly, Father." He hesitated. "And, Father, I choose to forgive Paulina of her sin against me. Please forgive her as well, Father. In Jesus' Name. Amen."

A guard approached Luca's cell. "Your dinner." The guard opened the little wooden food door and passed a bowl of mush toward Luca. The guard followed it with a cup of water.

"Thank you." Luca took the bowl and the cup and placed them on the bench.

"This will be your only meal until tomorrow morning, at which point I will collect your bowl and cup and give you fresh ones." The guard turned to go.

"Excuse me, sir?" Luca called after him.

"Yes?"

"Is there any way of letting my wife know that I am here?"

The guard hesitated. "I will see what I can do for you."

"Thank you, sir! Thank you very much!"

Luca sat down on the bench, barely able to see the food before him. He thanked God for his provision then ate the meager rations. The concoction was bitter in his mouth and difficult to swallow, and it left a residue of acidity that curdled in his stomach, nauseating him. The water was not much better.

As Luca finished his meal, the sound of a large door closing shut resounded in the air.

The prisoner across from him answered Luca's unspoken question. "The night door. Once that's shut, we're doubly imprisoned."

A pall of despair settled over Luca. What if he were found guilty of the theft? What if he were convicted? What if he spent years in prison?

He fought the horrendous thought. No, surely a court of law would see that he was innocent. Surely his good reputation would carry him.

Surely Paulina, as evil as she was, would recant and admit the truth.

But would she? Would a woman as wicked as she have an ounce of decency left in her bones?

God, please reveal the truth. Please, Father.

Every fiber of his being cried out to God. *Lord, You know I am innocent. Why is this happening?*

But in the stillness of the night, he heard only silence.

* * * *

Long after closing time, Will sat in his office, staring through the large window at the Brooklyn Bridge. The shadows of night hung heavy over the imposing structure that spanned the East River, obscuring its twin Gothic towers that stood serene, like a strong fortress in the midst of an uncertain world. Arc lamps lit the promenade filled with carriages and buggies that, from a distance, looked like so many ants marching across the massive expanse. People going home from a day of hard work or to Manhattan Island for a night of entertainment.

The events of the past afternoon had shaken Will to the core. The empty vault, the search for the missing moneybox among the employees, and its discovery at Luca's workstation had left Will stunned and despondent. Worst of all was his disappointment at seeing Luca Tonetta, a man he'd grown to trust, betray him.

But why? Will had given the immigrant a job sight unseen and solely on the recommendation of his friend Giulio. Luca had proven faithful enough. Beyond faithful, even. Will had never had occasion to reprimand him, and he'd produced twice the finished quota as the others in the workshop. In Will's estimation, Luca Tonetta was a man of sterling character.

Until today.

Tears stung Will's eyes. Why the tears, he did not know. Maybe Luca had represented for Will the hope of a day when the world would be good. When men would do the right thing simply because it was the right thing to do.

But why should Will think Luca any different from other men? Why should Will hope in the possibility of good in the world?

His own life was a betrayal. A betrayal of everything Mama had taught him about loving God and loving one's neighbor.

"Willie Boy." Mama's tender voice rang in Will's ears. "There was only one man in the whole world who was good. His name was Jesus. Be like Him."

Mama's words surfaced from his ten-year-old memory. *"His name was Jesus."*

Will turned away from the window and swiveled his chair toward his desk. Maybe it was time he got back in touch with this man named Jesus. Maybe it was time he obeyed Mama's words.

Maybe it was time he turned over a new leaf.

Chapter Seventeen

An hour passed, and Luca had not yet returned home from work. Maria's stomach tensed. What could have happened to him?

Dreadful thoughts bombarded her mind. Thoughts about Luca and Paulina. She forced them away.

"Nico, please play with your sisters while I put the food away and clean up the kitchen."

"Yes, Mama." Nico took Valeria and Anna by the hands and led them to the far corner of the room. "Mama, where is Papa?"

Maria sighed. "I don't know, son. I thought he'd be here by now. Frankly, I'm getting a bit concerned." When would Luca be back? It was getting late, and she had to bathe the little ones and put them to bed.

"Do you want me to go upstairs to check at the workshop?"

"It's after ten o'clock. The shop is likely closed by now." She hesitated. "If you stay with Valeria and Anna, I will go myself. Perhaps someone is still there who can give me some information."

She removed her apron, folded it, and placed it on the kitchen table. After giving the girls a stern warning to obey Nico, she slipped out of her flat, locked the door behind her, and hastened toward the stairwell leading to the workshop on the floor above.

All was dark except for a light shining under the door of Mr. Dempsey's office. Taking a deep breath, she knocked on the door.

"Who is it?" Will's voice echoed through the door.

"It's Maria Tonetta, Luca Tonetta's wife."

In a moment, the door opened. Will stood before her, his face white, his eyes glistening.

Maria wrung her hands. "I am sorry to disturb you, Mr. Dempsey, but I have come looking for Luca. He has not yet returned home, and I am worried."

Compassion filled Will's eyes. "Luca will not be coming home tonight."

Maria's heart froze. "Is he working late? Has something happened to him? Is he all right?" The questions rushed forth out of her heart.

"Luca is in prison. He was arrested this afternoon for stealing money that belonged to our company. He was not permitted to contact you before the police took him to jail." He lowered his gaze and then raised it again. "I was planning to notify you myself once the police gave me leave."

"But there must be some mistake! Luca would never steal anything. He is a man of honor and integrity." Bursting into sobs, Maria crumpled to the floor and buried her face in her hands. She grabbed Will's ankles. "Please, Mr. Dempsey. Please. Save my Luca. He is innocent, I tell you."

Will drew her up to her feet. "I will do whatever I can. I promise you." He patted both her hands. "Now go home to your children."

She nodded.

"And pray like you've never prayed before."

* * * *

The guard's voice awakened Luca from a restless sleep. "There is someone here to see you."

Luca rose and hastened to the cold, rough bars of his prison cell and wrapped his fingers tightly around them. In the darkness, he could barely discern the two figures moving toward him. Maria approached, followed by another prison guard.

"Luca!" Maria ran the last few steps toward him and wrapped her fingers over his.

He squeezed her fingers with everything in him. "Maria! Oh, Maria! Seeing you revives me. Where are the children? And do they know?"

"I left them with Enza Addevico. They know nothing yet." Her gaze pierced his. "Luca, tell me what happened. I have been worried sick."

The guards remained present as Luca explained the incidents of the day before. "So, when the police found the money in my garment bin, I was arrested for theft."

"But you are innocent!"

"I know that, and you know that, but the challenge comes with convincing a jury of my innocence." Luca caressed Maria's cheek.

"How long will you be here?"

"I don't know. Until my trial, which, I've been told, should take place in about a month."

"You'll be here over Christmas." Maria choked back a sob.

"Unfortunately, yes. I was asked if I wanted to post bail, but I don't have the money."

"I could try to get it for you."

"How, dear one?"

She shook her head. "I don't know. I could figure out a way."

"At this point, the only thing we can do is pray. God is my Defender, and He will not forsake me." Luca wiped away the tears streaming down Maria's cheeks.

"Your time is up, Mrs. Tonetta." The guard's voice was stern but polite.

Luca clung to Maria's fingers, only to have their hands

separated by the guard.

"I said, 'Your time is up!'"

"I love you, Luca." Maria's eyes held his."

"I love you, too, dear one."

Luca's gaze followed Maria as she left. Her visit had both revived him and depressed him. At the sound of the clicking door lock, he sank onto the wooden bench and wept.

* * * *

The light of a new day filtered through her balcony door as Paulina lay wide-awake on her bed. She stared at the ceiling above her, mindlessly tracing the molding running along the edges of the ceiling. Following it over and over again, round and round the room. Like her life, it was going nowhere.

She hadn't slept the entire night, her conscience stricken with guilt at having falsely accused an innocent man. She'd told Luca she had no conscience. She'd lied. Not only did she have a conscience, but never had it tormented her as it tormented her now.

She rolled over on her side. Luca's anguished face flashed before her. He knew. He knew she'd planted the money in his garment bin. He even knew the reason she'd done so.

Yet, he hadn't said a word.

He would leave the human judging to the courts.

And the eternal judging to God.

She buried her face in her hands. *God.* She'd sinned against Him. And now she was afraid. Afraid of His just punishment.

Sinning with her body had not bothered her. It was, after all, related to love, wasn't it? But betraying another human being by falsely accusing him of a crime he did not commit?

That was a despicable act committed only by the most depraved.

She swallowed the lump in her throat.

And what of Luca's wife and children? What kind of person would hurt a mother and her children? Why hadn't Paulina thought of them before committing her deplorable act?

She'd brought suffering not only on an innocent man but also on his innocent family.

How far she'd come from the devoted little girl she'd left behind in Russia! The child who'd accompanied her grandmother to church every week. Who'd prayed to a God she didn't know but whom she'd wanted desperately to know.

What had happened to her?

And where was God now?

Truth be told, she'd abandoned Him. Of her own free will. No wonder he'd abandoned her. She'd have done the same thing if she were God.

She rose from the bed, walked toward the balcony door, and opened it. A rush of cold air brushed her face, bringing her to full wakefulness. Overhead, gray clouds swept over the tenement houses across the street, blocking out the sun.

As she closed the balcony doors, a thought struck her. She would take a trip to Russia. Until after Luca's trial. No one suspected her of the crime. She'd have time to escape and, if she were implicated at a later date, she would remain hidden in her homeland.

She would tell Will she needed to go to Moscow right away because her great-aunt was dying. Paulina would book passage today.

And never return.

Chapter Eighteen

Will sat at his usual place at the counter of O'Malley's Tavern, downing his third glass of whiskey. The place was crowded with dozens of men chattering in friendly banter as they whittled away their week's earnings. In the background, two banjo players strummed a catchy, ragtime song, America's latest musical rage. The tapping of feet, the drumming of fingers, and the clanking of glasses filled the air.

Despite the hilarity around him, Will sat oblivious to his surroundings, burdened as he was with Luca's recent charge of theft. Something didn't sit right with Will. For one thing, Paulina seemed certain Luca was the thief. Her visit to his office earlier that day had left him more suspicious than ever about her implication in the theft. Especially since she'd requested time off to go visit her dying great-aunt in Russia. This was the first Will had heard that Paulina even *had* a great-aunt in Russia.

But he had no tangible evidence to support his suspicions. Only a gut feeling that was growing stronger and stronger by the minute.

He took another swig of whiskey, allowing the warm, pain-numbing liquid to slide down his throat.

"Having a bad day, Will?" O'Malley stood before him, wiping the counter top with a wet rag.

"You could say that."

"Heard about the theft at your place. Too bad."

Will looked up at him. "Word sure gets around fast in these parts. You'd think the city would keep to itself."

"Well, if you look at Brooklyn like a bunch of tight, little neighborhoods instead of a big city, then no wonder word spreads fast."

"Yeah, I guess you're right."

O'Malley rubbed a stubborn spot to the right of Will. "So, what's the latest on the thief?"

Will rubbed his hand across his chin. "Wish I could tell you. He goes to trial next week."

"Officer Casey McBride stops in for an occasional drink after finishing his beat. He's the one who told me about the theft."

"When?"

"Just before you came in."

"Maybe he'll know the latest scoop on the trial, too." Will chugged down the last of his drink, put a few coins on the counter in payment, and left.

A cold rush of night air hit him as he left the tavern and headed straight for the police station. He'd get the latest scoop on the theft straight from Office McBride himself, or, if he were off duty, from Captain Pete Schreiber.

. Maybe they'd been trying to get ahold of him.

Will propped up his coat collar around his neck to ward off the icy wind. Snow flurries filled the air, falling like white diamonds to the ground below. A little child ahead of him tried to catch them with his tongue, shouting with delight as they fell on it.

All around Will, people scurried to their destinations. Women carrying shopping bags filled with Christmas gifts. Men carrying large briefcases on their way home from work. Factory workers clinging to lunch pails as they hurried to catch a train or a bus.

He rounded the corner to the police precinct. An old man in tattered rags sat on the curb in front of the precinct, holding a tin cup in his hand. Will reached into his pocket, withdrew a couple of coins, and tossed them into the cup.

The man smiled at the clang of the coins against the tin of the cup.

Will teetered only slightly as he entered the precinct. Except for Captain Schreiber sitting at the main desk, the place was empty.

Captain Schreiber looked up. "So, what brings you here, Will Dempsey?"

Will forced a smile. "I didn't think you'd recognize me, Captain."

Captain Schreiber laughed. "I'd recognize you a mile away, Dempsey. Guys like you keep guys like me in business." He laughed again.

"Not very funny."

"Okay. Okay. I didn't mean to offend you. In my line of work, a good laugh is a necessity."

"Yes, but not at my expense."

"Well, aren't you in a good mood today!"

"I've seen better days."

Captain Schreiber softened up on him. "Okay, so what can I do for you?"

"I was just down at O'Malley's Tavern and Brian O'Malley told me you had a scoop on the Tonetta guy who stole the money from my workshop."

Captain Schreiber narrowed his eyes. "What else did O'Malley say?"

"Nothing much else."

Captain Schreiber pulled out his handkerchief and blew his nose. "Word sure gets around fast, don't it?"

"So, it's the truth then. You think Tonetta's guilty."

"Yeah, it's the truth. He's the best suspect we have to go on at this point. He was the one who had the wooden box of money in his garment bin."

"But how can you be sure he put it there?"

"We can't, but we have nothing else to go on. At least, not at this point in the investigation."

"So that justifies your charging an innocent man?"

Captain Schreiber stared at Will. "How do you know he's innocent?"

"I just have a hunch, that's all."

"Look, Will, you're right. That's all a hunch is—a hunch. And nothing more."

"But sometimes you've got to follow a hunch."

"What makes you think your hunch is worth following?"

"I've known Luca for only a couple of months, but during those months, he's been an honest worker. He goes the extra mile, and he refuses to back down on his principles. He even refused to work on Sundays and told me that if I insisted he work on Sundays, he'd quit and find another job. He's got a real respect for God."

Captain Schreiber shook his finger at Will. "The perfect red herring for a crime. A man who's so good no one would ever think he was the guilty one. The perfect cover-up. Maybe Mr. Tonetta has been setting you up for a long time."

"I just can't believe it of him. Another thing. There's this woman who sits across from him who's been trying to seduce him, but he keeps resisting her advances."

"What's her name?"

"Paulina Ivanov." Should Will divulge his personal relationship with Paulina?

"How well do you know her?"

Will lowered his eyes then raised them again. "Better than I should."

Captain Schreiber raised an eyebrow. "I see." He leaned forward in his chair and locked his gaze onto Will's. "Looks to me like you've given me more fuel for the fire. I need to talk with this Paulina woman." He nodded slowly. "Your hunch may be right after all."

"She just left for Russia to visit her dying great-aunt."

Captain Schreiber cocked an eyebrow. "Oh, she did, did she?" He rubbed his chin. "Now isn't that a coincidence?"

Will looked him squarely in the eye. "I told you I had a hunch."

* * * *

The morning after Maria's visit, Luca awoke to the sound of the prison guard calling to him through the bars. "Tonetta, wake up. Your attorney will be here soon to talk with you."

Luca strained to shift from sleep to wakefulness. The hard, narrow bench had made a good night's sleep impossible. He'd lain awake till the wee hours of the morning, praying, revisiting the whole theft incident, wondering what the future held.

He rose, attended to his personal needs, and then awaited the arrival of the attorney. Because of Luca's lack of money, a public attorney had been assigned to his defense.

The guard returned with the attorney at his side. He unlocked the cell to allow the attorney to enter and then locked it again.

"Hello. My name is Edward Wilkes." He wore a black suit with a white shirt and a navy blue silk tie. A dark, well-cropped beard covered the lower half of his face, extending from his upper lip to his chin. Wire-rimmed glasses covered a pair of brilliant blue eyes that shone in the opaque darkness of the cell.

The attorney smiled and extended a hand toward Luca. "I will be serving as your defense attorney at your upcoming trial."

Luca returned the handshake. "Thank you, Mr Wilkes."

Luca liked him immediately.

Mr. Wilkes took a seat on the bench next to Luca. "Now,

tell me your side of the story."

For the next hour, Luca explained the theft from his perspective, repeatedly denying his guilt. All the while, Wilkes wrote furiously on the legal pad he'd brought with him. When the attorney inquired if Luca had any idea who had stolen the money and who might have anything against him, Luca mentioned Paulina. He explained her continual attempts to seduce him, attempts he had aggressively resisted, much to Paulina's dismay.

"So, she is the only person you can think of who has an axe to grind against you?"

Luca furrowed his brows. "I'm sorry. What do you mean by 'an axe to grind'?"

The attorney chuckled and then explained to Luca the meaning of the English idiom.

Luca smiled in return. "Yes. Paulina is the only one who has an axe to grind."

The attorney nodded then rose. "Very well, Mr. Tonetta. We have a good chance of winning this case. But, of course, we won't know how things go until the day of the trial."

Luca stood. "Yes, of course. Do you know yet when the trial will be?"

"It's scheduled for next Monday morning."

A week away. Thank God the ordeal would be over soon.

"Thank you again for your kindness in helping me. I wish I could pay you."

"Not at all. It is my pleasure to serve you in this capacity." The attorney called for the guard who was standing nearby. "Good day, Mr. Tonetta."

"Good day to you, too. I will be praying for you."

The attorney looked into Luca's eyes. "And I for you."

Peace flooded Luca's soul.

The guard unlocked the cell to allow the attorney to leave.

Luca had a sudden urge to follow him out of the cell. But before he could dismiss the thought, the guard shut the barred door and turned the key in the lock.

The clicking of the key in the lock rang in the dank air, leaving Luca alone again in the silence of his grief.

* * * *

The Friday before Luca's trial, the prison guard appeared at Luca's cell. "This letter was forwarded here for you."

Luca rose and reached through the bars. "Thank you. I wasn't aware I could receive mail."

"One letter a month." The guard nodded toward the letter. "There you have it."

As the guard turned to leave, Luca thanked him again and then tore open the seal. His heart leapt. The letter was from Jonathan Mitchell, the missionary who had led him to Christ.

Dear Luca,

At long last, I am responding to your most welcome letter that reached me while I was still in Japan. How happy I was to hear from you and to learn that you are in the United States! Welcome to America!

By the time you receive this, I, too, will have returned to America and would like very much to visit you. As Providence would have it, I am scheduled to spend three weeks at the Brooklyn Mission in January. Perhaps we can meet there to renew our acquaintance, to pray, and to discuss ways that you can fulfill your call to preach the Gospel in America.

I trust you are doing well, and I look forward to hearing from you again soon.

Your faithful brother in Christ,

Jonathan Mitchell

Luca sighed as he folded the letter and laid it on the wooden bench. How would Jonathan react when he learned that Luca was in prison on charges of theft? A criminal record would destroy all chances of his joining Jonathan in preaching the Gospel.

Luca sank to his knees. A deep sense of shame threatened to overtake him at the realization that his credibility as a man of integrity was now gone. Even if the court proved him innocent, a black spot would forever remain on his name. Who would ever trust him again? Who would ever believe him again?

Worst of all, who would believe the Gospel coming out of the mouth of a man considered to be a criminal?

Luca bowed his head. "Father God, I don't understand what is going on. I don't understand the reason You are allowing this great trial in my life. But I submit to Your will, Father. I trust you with my life, with Maria's life, and with the lives of our children. You take care of the birds of the air. Take care of my little flock. I pray in Jesus' Name. Amen."

A deep sense of peace flooded Luca's soul. He rested his head on the bench and fell fast asleep.

Chapter Nineteen

The morning of the trial, Maria rose before dawn. Her head ached with the prospect of what lay before Luca and her. Ever since Luca's charge and imprisonment, she'd been praying fervently for his vindication. Today would tell if God had answered her prayers.

She washed and dressed and then prepared breakfast for the children. Enza had agreed to take Valeria and Anna for the day. Nico would accompany Maria to the courthouse to attend the trial.

The Kings County Courthouse stood only a few blocks from their tenement house. With Nico at her side, Maria hastened toward the old, stately building at the southwest corner of the intersection of Joralemon Street and Boerum Place. Its majestic cupola, framed against a bright blue winter sky, inspired awe. In front of the cupola, at the uppermost angle of the triangular façade, an American flag waved proudly in the breeze.

Maria took a deep breath. *The land of the free and the home of the brave.* Would Luca's trial prove the truth of that famous epithet for their new homeland?

She found the main door and entered the building. An attendant directed her and Nico to the room where Luca's trial would be held.

As they entered the courtroom, Maria's heart clenched. Several people had already arrived, most of them reporters. With pencils and paper ready in hand, they awaited the arrival of the defendant, the defense attorney, the plaintiff, the prosecuting attorney, and the judge.

Maria and Nico took a seat in the front row. Her heart pounded wildly as she waited for the proceedings to begin. In a few moments, the doors to the courtroom opened, and the prosecuting attorney entered together with Will Dempsey. Shortly thereafter, the defense attorney arrived, flanked by Luca.

Maria's gaze found his. In that instant, their hearts touched.

Following close behind Luca were Jake Goldberg and Gennaro Cappadona. Paulina was nowhere in sight.

The jury filed in and took its place to the right of the judge's bench and in full view of the witness stand.

At the appearance of the judge, the entire court rose. He was a tall man, imposing in presence, and wearing a long black robe that set a tone of solemnity and seriousness. The judge ordered the people to be seated.

At the strike of the judge's gavel, the room came to attention.

Maria prayed silently as the proceedings began.

* * * *

Luca's stomach churned as witness after witness came to the stand. Most were fellow employees at the Dempsey Workshop. Some attested to Luca's guilt, others, to his innocence.

Finally, Luca himself was called to the witness stand. The cross-examination by the prosecutor presented language challenges that Giulio, prior to the trial, had offered to interpret. At the end of the grueling interrogation, Luca gave an impassioned plea, declaring his innocence. He then returned to his seat beside his attorney and waited.

The judge then called Paulina to the witness stand.

"Your Honor, Paulina Ivanov is not here. She is in Russia visiting her dying great-aunt." The prosecutor's voice echoed throughout the large hall.

The judge shifted in his chair. "But she was issued a subpoena, was she not?"

"Yes, Your Honor, but she left before receiving it."

The judge leaned back in his chair and folded his hands over his chest. "Now that presents a problem, doesn't it? How long will she be gone?"

"Indefinitely, your Honor."

A light chatter arose in the courtroom. The judge struck the gavel. "Order in the court!" He turned toward Luca's attorney. "Do you have any other witnesses?"

"No, your Honor."

The judge grew pensive. "Very well. Since Paulina Ivanov is out of the country with no foreseeable date of return, we will proceed without her. I order the court dismissed for the jury's deliberation. Court will resume when the jury reaches a verdict." With that, the judge struck his gavel once again.

Luca signaled to Maria who, with Nico, hastened to approach him. Luca took both her hands. "Are you all right?"

She nodded. "The question is, 'Are you all right?'"

"As well as can be expected."

An hour later, the court reassembled.

The judge struck the gavel. "Will the jury please give its verdict?"

Luca's heart pounded as he held his breath. His family's entire future rested on the jury's decision. Twelve people literally held Luca's life, Maria's life, and the lives of their children in their hands.

He leaned forward, his hands folded on the table in front of him, every muscle in his body tense with anticipation.

Mr. Wilkes mirrored Luca's position.

The spokesman for the jury rose to his feet.

"What is your verdict?" The judge's voice boomed

across the large room.

"Your Honor, this jury has determined that the defendant, Luca Tonetta, is guilty of theft as charged!"

Luca's gaze flew to Maria. As their eyes met, their hearts joined in death.

* * * *

Back in his cell, Luca fell to his knees in despair. The judge had given him a sentence of five years, with a possible opportunity for parole, pending good behavior, in four. Sobs wracked Luca's body as the full implication of the sentence took root in his mind.

After several moments, he stood. Turning toward the wall, he startled at the sight of his stubbled face in the tiny metal reflector plate that hung over the washbasin. His eyes had lost their light. His face, worn and wrinkled from having spent a month in this medieval dungeon, looked like that of an old man.

He took a deep breath. What had become of him? Where was the strapping young man who had set foot on American soil only a short three months before? The optimistic dreamer who had held the world in his hands? Once strong and vibrant, he now looked like an old man fast approaching death.

Worse yet, what had become of his family? Of his dream of a better life? Of his mission to preach the Gospel?

This was not a better life. Not the life he'd imagined when he'd decided to come to America. This life was a nightmare.

Sure, he'd expected to work hard. To be uncomfortable for a little while as they faced the challenges of adapting to a new culture.

To pay a price for achieving success.

He'd traded the beautiful lush landscape of *Bella Terra*

for a rat-infested tenement house in Brooklyn. A tenement house filled with the stench of garbage left out in the heat. With the incessant buzzing of flies covered with droppings from that garbage. The muffled weeping of his wife in her pillow at night. As though she could hide her despair from him. And the sad faces of his children, trying to make the best out of a deplorable situation.

Now he found himself imprisoned in a medieval dungeon for a crime he hadn't committed.

He swallowed hard. "Lord, did I miss Your will? Was I deceived into thinking that my selfish ambition was Your voice? Did I follow my own foolish dreams and not Yours?" His deepest fear was missing God's will through his own pride and selfish ambition. What if Jesus had gone His own way? Done His own will?

Refused to obey the Father's will?

O God, help me!

He lowered his eyes and shook his head. What kind of a man was he? What despicable person had he become to put his family through such suffering, including an arrest and an indictment for a crime he hadn't committed?

No. He hadn't expected this. Not in his wildest dreams had he ever expected this.

He swallowed hard. What would Maria and the children do now? Surely, they couldn't survive without his income. Nico was still a boy. He couldn't earn enough to support the family. Luca would have to send them all back to Sicily while he remained here to die in this dungeon all alone.

He leaned his hands on the edge of the washbasin and swallowed hard. He'd never been this close to despair. This close to giving up.

This close to wanting to die.

"Lord, did I miss Your will? Is this the reason we're being punished? Was I deceived into thinking that my selfish ambition was Your voice? Did I follow my own foolish dreams and not Yours?"

Hot tears stung his eyes as a sob rose to his throat. His deepest fear had come true. He'd missed God's will for his life. In so doing, he'd ruined the dearest, most precious people in his life—his wife and his children—through his own selfishness. And he'd done so through his own prideful and selfish ambition. How could he ever make amends for his horrendous behavior?

Tears streamed down his cheeks. Only a miracle could save his family.

He lowered his face into his trembling hands and wept bitterly. All the pent-up anguish of the past month poured out of his broken soul, releasing the salt of bitterness onto his lips.

As he wept bitterly, he heard these words in his spirit: *Did I ever say following Me would be easy?*

No, Lord. You didn't.

But know this, My son. It will be so worth it.

A spark of hope ignited in Luca's soul. He hadn't missed God's will at all. Just as Jesus hadn't missed God's will when He stumbled up Calvary Hill to His Crucifixion.

If even the Lord wondered about His own destiny as Savior, surely Luca's questions were understandable. No matter how bleak things looked, there was still hope because of Jesus. Together with Him, Luca would get through this. His family would get through this.

Luca would cling to that truth.

A voice behind him caught him by surprise. "Papa?"

He turned to find four-year-old Valeria standing outside the cell with Maria, Anna, and Nico.

Luca's heart leapt for joy.

Valeria extended her little hand through the bars, a smile on her four-year-old face and a drawing in her hand. "Papa, this is for you."

His eyes brimming with tears, Luca stooped down to her level and took the drawing from her hand. It showed a stick man walking into a house. "What is this, little one?"

"It's a picture of you coming home. Will you hang it on your wall until you do come home, Papa?"

Oh, the faith of a little child! A lump formed in Luca's throat. "Yes. I will hang it on my cell wall until I come home."

Valeria's face burst into a brilliant smile.

Luca pressed his cheek against the bars and placed his little girl's hand upon it. "O my precious little girl. You have no idea how much your drawing means to me."

Valeria pulled back from him and laughed. "Now watch, Papa. God will bring you home to us soon."

Luca's heart wrenched as tears spilled onto his face. "Yes, my precious little one, He will. He most certainly will."

And in the deepest recesses of his heart, Luca was absolutely sure God would.

Chapter Twenty

Summer had just begun in Brooklyn when Paulina's ship arrived at the East River port. After six months in Russia, she'd decided to return home to come clean of her crime. Being away had given her a fresh perspective on the depravity of her life. Her conscience could no longer bear the tormenting guilt of her sin and the unbearable strain of living a lie. No matter what happened, she would confess.

And, truth be told, she missed Will. Missed him terribly. But would she still find him interested in her? Or had he found someone else in the interim?

She disembarked from the large vessel and made her way to customs. After her belongings were quickly examined, she re-entered the bustling city that had been her home for so many years.

Her first stop would be to Luca's flat. She wanted to tell Luca's wife the truth and, if possible, ask her forgiveness. From there, she would go to Will to tell him the truth and then, finally, to the police.

The horse and buggy stopped directly in front of her old tenement house. Placing a coin in the driver's palm, she asked him to wait while she paid a short visit. She climbed up to the third floor and found Luca's flat. Her heart beating, she knocked on the door.

A beautiful young woman, with sorrowful eyes, opened the door. "Yes?"

"Hello. I am looking for Maria Tonetta."

"Yes. I am Maria Tonetta. Please come in."

Paulina entered and stood in front of the open doorway.

Maria motioned toward a chair. "Won't you sit down?"

"Only for a moment. My driver is waiting for me outside."

Maria offered Paulina a chair at the kitchen table and sat down next to her.

"My name is Paulina Ivanov."

Maria's face turned pale as her eyes narrowed.

"I used to work with your husband at the workshop upstairs."

Maria nodded. "Yes, I know who you are." She clipped her words.

Paulina struggled to continue in the face of Maria's obvious displeasure. "I have been in Russia for six months, tormented with something I must tell you." Paulina lowered her gaze.

Maria crossed her arms. "Please go on."

Paulina looked up, tears spilling on to her cheeks. "I have come to tell you that your husband is innocent of the theft at the workshop. I am the guilty one. I am the thief who stole the money."

Maria'a gaze softened slightly. "But why?"

Did Paulina dare tell Luca's wife the truth about her former feelings toward Luca? Yes, she must confess everything in order to be totally clean. "I tried several times to seduce your husband, but he always resisted me. It made me so angry that I decided to seek vengeance by implicating him in a crime." Tears streamed down her face as she lowered her gaze. "I am so sorry! So very, very sorry! Can you ever forgive me?"

Maria took Paulina's hands. "I forgive you. And I know Luca will forgive you, too."

Paulina looked up. "But how can you forgive me? I have destroyed your lives."

Maria smiled. "We can forgive you because of Jesus

Christ. Do you know Him?"

"No. But I would like to know the God who can cause you to forgive the likes of me."

"You can know Jesus now by accepting Him into your life." Maria led Paulina in a prayer to receive Christ as her personal Savior and Lord.

As Paulina prayed, she was filled with peace and a deep knowing that her sins had been washed away. "Thank you. Thank you so very much!"

Maria nodded as tears welled up in her eyes.

"And now, I must go right away to confess to Mr. Dempsey and then to the police. I wanted to come here first because I owed it to you as Luca's wife to ask for your forgiveness." Paulina rose to go.

As she left, Maria embraced her. "You have no idea what you have just done for us. May God bless you for your courage."

"You are a blessed woman to have such a Godly husband."

"I pray that God will give you a Godly husband as well."

Paulina squeezed Maria's hand. "Thank you. But only if I don't have to spend the rest of my life in jail. But if I do, I know Jesus will be with me." Paulina smiled through her tears.

"May God grant you mercy."

"He already has." With that, Paulina left, free in spirit for the first time in her life.

* * * *

A brilliant sun graced the early June sky the morning of Luca's release. Maria and the children had arrived bright and early with a new set of clothes to celebrate the wonderful occasion. Now, holding her hand in his, Luca pushed through the door of the prison into the sweet blessing of freedom.

At the sight of the huge crowd standing outside the prison, his heart stirred. Waving and cheering, they shouted his name. His eyes filled with tears and his heart welled up with gratitude at the sight of so many people who believed in his innocence. He looked up to Heaven and offered a prayer of thanks.

Paulina's confession had made him a free man again.

Reporters from various newspapers lined the steps, shooting question after question at Luca. But he declined to answer, other than to say he'd left written comments on his release with his attorney. His only immediate goal now was to get home.

With Maria and his three children by his side, he made his way down the flight of steps to the waiting horse and buggy. Giulio stood holding the door open, prepared to usher them into the vehicle to take them home to their flat. There, Luca would finally enjoy that special Italian meal Giulio had promised to cook for him back in Sicily.

So very long ago, it seemed.

The weather had grown warm in Brooklyn. Summer was just around the corner, bringing with it bluer skies and the fragrance of lilacs and roses. Luca took a deep breath of the precious air, so different from the putrid odors of the dark, dank prison. Suffering made precious the things one used to take for granted.

Six months in prison had left him a changed man. A better man.

A more thankful man.

Within that dungeon of despair, he'd met his Lord in a deeper way and come to appreciate the true meaning of freedom in Christ. Man could shackle the body, but only sin could shackle the soul. A follower of Christ was truly free no matter where he was, for freedom was an internal state more than an external one.

Giulio smiled broadly, his eyes brimming with tears, as Luca approached the buggy.

Luca grabbed him in a tight embrace. "Thank you, my friend! Thank you!"

As Luca entered the buggy, a brown-and-white puppy jumped into his arms and started licking his face.

Luca laughed. "What's this?"

Nico was at his Papa's side. "It's my new puppy. *Signor* Genova's dog had a litter of puppies, and he gave me one. I've named him Pippo the Second."

Tears rushed to Luca's eyes. "That is a fine name, son."

Nico pressed into Luca with a tight hug.

"Papa, sit next to me!" Anna tugged on Luca's arm.

"No, sit next to me!" Valeria contended for her father's attention.

Luca laughed. "I can sit next to both of you. One on my right, and one on my left."

"But what about Mama? Where will she sit?"

"She can sit across from me where I can look into her beautiful, dark eyes." Luca's gaze locked onto Maria's. In her eyes he saw the profound depth of her love for him and the deep joy that he was with her once again.

Nico stood by the open door of the buggy. "I'll sit next to Giulio so he can teach me how to handle one of these things."

Luca tousled his son's hair. "Then you can take us around town," Luca teased. He grew solemn. "I missed you, Nico."

The boy's eyes filled with tears. "I missed you, too, Papa."

As Nico closed the door of the buggy, Luca took Maria's hand. "I thought this day would never come. But, thank God, now it's here."

"We have much to catch up on, Luca. But first, I want

you to get some rest."

"I will. But only after we feast on that wonderful meal that Giulio has prepared for us. The best Italian meal this side of the Atlantic."

Maria laughed. "Yes. That was his promise, wasn't it?"

"Then after I get some rest, we will discuss where we go from here."

"The Lord will direct our paths. He's done so this far. He will not fail us."

"The first thing I will need to do is find a job. I don't think Mr. Dempsey will take me back after I drew such negative attention to his workshop."

"What about the Mission?"

"But that's a volunteer position."

"Not always. I recently heard that the current director will be resigning soon to take a position at another mission in Chicago. Perhaps you could apply for his job."

The thought ignited passion in Luca's soul. Was this the opportunity he'd been praying for? To preach the Gospel full-time in America?

"That sounds like a wonderful idea! I will apply then leave the results in the Lord's hands."

Maria smiled. "May the Lord's will be done."

A crowd of friends greeted Luca with cheers as he entered his flat where Giulio had brought the promised meal. "Welcome home, Luca! Praise the Lord for His faithfulness!"

The appetizing aroma of garlic and olive oil filled the air, mingling with Giulio's homemade pasta. As Luca sat down once again at his place at the table, surrounded by faithful friends, his heart stirred with gratitude. "Thank You, Heavenly Father, for Your many blessings. Most of all, thank You for setting us free. For whom the Son sets free is free, indeed!"

That night, for the first time in six months, Luca slept in

his own bed. Never had he been so happy. Never had he loved his Lord so much!

* * * *

From his first-floor office window at the Brooklyn Mission, Luca gazed out at the busy street crowded with the poor and the homeless lined up outside the Mission and awaiting a meal. Faces young and old, saddened by suffering, gazed back at him with empty eyes and even emptier souls. How his heart ached for them! They were broken people. Outcasts rejected by society.

People loved by God.

And how thankful he was finally to be preaching the Gospel to these poorest of the poor in America! He would write to Don Franco to tell him about the wonderful opportunity the Lord had given him.

Rays of early summer sunshine filtered through the office window, casting long afternoon shadows on the concrete floor. A potted red geranium, compliments of Maria, sat on the windowsill, adding a touch of color to the plain, gray-walled office. Under the window, an old wooden file cabinet stored purchase orders for food and supplies used to minister to those who came to the Mission. Formerly an old warehouse, the Mission now housed a large dining room, a kitchen, and two large rooms—one for men and one for women—lined with cots where the homeless could sleep.

The Mission was growing rapidly, and many souls were coming to Christ. Luca couldn't be happier. Had it not been for the recommendation of his missionary friend, Jonathan Mitchell, he would never have been offered the job of Mission Director. It was the job for which he had been created. The job in which he could best fulfill his destiny in Christ.

And the job that allowed him to work side by side with

Maria and his children. All of them regularly volunteered at the Mission, feeding the poor, sheltering the homeless, praying for their needs, and sharing the Gospel of salvation.

Luca turned toward his desk and sat down to review the day's agenda. There was much work to be done to ensure that the Mission could continue to provide food and shelter for the poor and homeless. Requests for donations fell to him as director. Any love offerings he received through speaking at churches were donated to the Mission's general fund. Maria helped with ordering supplies and seeing to it that the shelves were kept stocked. The facility needed repairs, and Luca would have to recruit more volunteers to help with the increasing numbers of indigent people who flocked to the Mission. One of his goals was to start discipleship classes for those who came to Christ as a result of their ministry.

There was much to do, but God would supply all their needs.

Maria opened his office door and entered, her face radiant with joy. "Luca, I have an amazing surprise. You will never guess what it is. Not in a million years."

Luca smiled. He hadn't seen Maria this happy in years. "What is the amazing surprise I will never guess?"

"Will Dempsey and Paulina Ivanov are here to see you."

Luca's heart lurched. "Really? You're right. This is an amazing surprise. I would never in a million years have guessed as much. Please show them in."

Maria returned a few moments later with Will and Paulina in tow. Luca rose from his desk and rushed around it to embrace his old boss. "Mr. Dempsey! What an honor to see you again!"

Mr. Dempsey smiled. "The honor is all mine, Luca."

Luca smiled and turned to Paulina. "And it is a blessing to see you, Paulina. Maria told me you are now a sister in Christ."

Purity now lit Paulina's eyes. Jesus had changed her. "Yes. I am now a sister in Christ. But one who needs to ask your forgiveness."

Luca waved a dismissive hand. "Forgiveness granted. Please sit down."

Will spoke. "You will be surprised to learn that I, too, have come to Christ." He turned toward Paulina. "Via the influence of this remarkable woman."

Luca's heart rejoiced. "Praise the Lord! His mercies never cease!"

Will fingered his hat. "And I, too, need to ask your forgiveness, Luca. When Paulina told me the truth about the theft, I was stunned. But I decided not to press charges against her." Will smiled. "Instead, I decided to marry her." He chuckled. "That's punishment enough for her." Will gave Paulina the precious look of an adoring fiancé.

A look she returned.

A shout of "Hallelujah" burst simultaneously from Luca's and Maria's lips. "This is nothing short of a miracle from God!" Luca lifted his hands in praise.

Will lowered his gaze and then raised it again. "We've come to ask you if you will be the best man in our wedding."

Luca's eyes filled with tears.

Paulina turned toward Maria. "And we would like you to be the matron of honor."

Luca leaned forward. "We are humbled by your invitation and gladly accept."

"Thank you." Will continued. "We would like to hold the wedding here, at the Mission Chapel, if possible."

Luca broke into a grin. "That would be most fitting."

Maria nodded. "Most fitting, indeed."

Paulina patted Will's hand. "Then it's settled. All we have to do is set the date."

After final arrangements were made, Will and Paulina left.

Luca took Maria into his arms. "How good is the Lord! Worthy of all our praise! He makes beauty out of ashes and sets the captives free."

Maria smiled. "And He does it all by the power of His love."

Luca kissed Maria. "And now, dear one, are you ready to turn the world upside down for Jesus?"

Maria snuggled into her husband's embrace. "I think you mean right-side up."

Luca laughed. "Yes, right-side up. What a wise wife I have!"

He looked through the window at the broken lives outside the Mission. Each one was searching for wholeness. Each one was searching for Jesus.

Little did Luca know that when he'd said farewell to Sicily, he'd said hello to true life.

He who loses his life for My sake shall find it.

For the first time in all of his life, Luca Tonetta had found true life.

END OF BOOK TWO

Return to Bella Terra

Book Three in *The Italian Chronicles* Series

A mother, her son, and the man who comes between them ...

The Madonna of Pisano

Book One in *The Italian Chronicles* Series

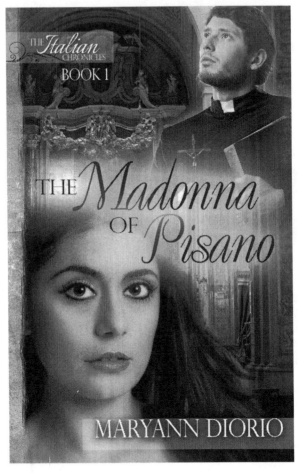

A young woman, a priest, and a secret that keeps them bitterly bound to each other...

AUTHOR'S NOTE

The seed for this story was planted more than one hundred years ago, when my paternal grandfather set sail for America. The outbreak of World War I shortly after his arrival prevented my grandmother and their two children from joining him as originally planned. Seven long, grueling years later, the ban on travel was lifted, and my grandparents were reunited.

This story was written as a tribute to them—and to all immigrants—who have endured the hardships of leaving their homelands, of deplorable conditions at sea, and of adapting to a new world that was often hostile and prejudiced against them.

More than that, however, this is the story of Christ's redemptive love and enduring faithfulness in the midst of the worst situations.

Because this book is a novel, much of the information has been modified to accommodate the story. Names have been altered, and circumstances and locations have been fictionalized. But its essential message remains the same: *Whoever loses his life for the sake of Jesus Christ will surely find it.*

QUESTIONS FOR GROUP DISCUSSION

NOTE: These questions may be used in a variety of ways, including book club or reading group discussions, in Bible-study groups dealing with the topic of forgiveness, and for personal meditation.

1. Luca struggled with discerning God's will. At times he wasn't sure he was hearing God's voice. Jesus said His sheep hear His voice. Have you ever struggled with hearing God's voice? What could be the problem when a Christ-Follower does not hear God's voice?

2. Maria wanted to submit to God's will, but she doubted that Luca was hearing God's voice. Is submitting to God's will a challenge for you? Is submitting to someone in authority over you a challenge for you? If so, why? What does the Bible say about submitting to those in authority over us?

3. Luca was imprisoned for a crime he did not commit. Jesus was crucified for sins He did not commit. What can we learn about Christ during the times we are wrongly accused? What can we learn about ourselves?

4. When Paulina admitted her guilt and asked Luca's forgiveness, he could have grown bitter and angry with her. Instead, he chose to forgive her. It has been said that forgiveness means living with the consequences of one's wrongdoing toward us. Are you paying the consequences for someone else's sin? If so, how are you handling that situation? Are you handling it the way Jesus would? If not, what can you change?

5. There are times when following Jesus seems to bring all kinds of trouble. These troubles could cause us to think that we missed God's will. Is it true that favor and blessing are always a sign of God's will? Could a person still be in God's will when everything seems to be going

wrong? Have you interpreted blessings as God's favor and problems as God's wrath? Is this an accurate interpretation of Scripture?

6. Luca was a tailor. This was his trade. But his calling was to preach the Gospel. The Apostle Paul was a tent-maker. But his calling was to preach the Gospel. How can we distinguish between our trade or profession and our calling? Are they ever one and the same? Are they always different?

7. Maria struggled to be content in her new surroundings. She missed her homeland and the house in which she'd lived all of her life. Have you ever struggled to be content in the midst of your circumstances? Why is contentment important? Why is living in the past a grave spiritual danger?

8. In Matthew 19: 29, Jesus said this: "And everyone who has left houses or brothers or sisters or father or mother or children or lands, for my name's sake, will receive a hundredfold and will inherit eternal life." How did this verse apply to Maria? Have you left family, children, or a home for the cause of Christ? What happened as a result?

9. Luca stood fast in the strength of Christ when facing temptation. What temptation are you facing? Are you facing it in God's grace and strength? If not, what do you need to change?

10. Will Dempsey eventually remembered the truths his mother taught him as a boy. Why is it important to instill God's truth into the hearts of our children? What does God mean when He says this in Isaiah 55: 11: "...so shall my word be that goes out from my mouth; it shall not return to me empty, but it shall accomplish that which I purpose, and shall succeed in the thing for which I sent it."

About the Author

MaryAnn's passion, as her registered trademark states, is to proclaim *Truth through Fiction®* because only truth will set people free (John 8:32). A widely published author of non-fiction, MaryAnn responded to God's call a few years ago to write fiction and has since published one novel, *The Madonna of Pisano*, two novellas, *A Christmas Homecoming* and *Surrender to Love*. She hopes her stories will entertain and point readers to Jesus Christ, the Truth Who alone can set them free.

Dr. MaryAnn holds a PhD in French and Comparative Literature from the University of Kansas. She lives in New Jersey with her husband Dominic, a retired physician. They are blessed with two lovely grown daughters, a wonderful son-in-law, and five rambunctious grandchildren. In her spare time, MaryAnn loves to read, paint, and make up silly songs for her grandchildren.

How to Live Forever

Eternal life is a free gift offered by God to anyone who chooses to accept it. All it takes is a sincere sorrow for your sins (contrition) and a quality decision to turn away from your sins (repentance) and begin living for God.

In John 3:3, Jesus said, "Unless one is born again, he cannot see the Kingdom of God." What does it mean to be "born again?" Simply put, it means to be restored to fellowship with God.

Man is made up of three parts: spirit, soul, and body (I Thessalonians 5:23). Your spirit is who you really are; your soul is comprised of your mind, your will, and your emotions; and your body is the housing for your spirit and your soul. You could call your body your "earth suit."

When we are born into this world, we are born with a spirit that is separated from God. As a result, it is a spirit without life because God alone is the Source of life. You may have heard this condition referred to as "original sin." Why is every human being born with a spirit separated from God? Because of the sin of our first parents, Adam and Eve.

I used to wonder why I had to suffer because of the sin of Adam and Eve. After all, I complained, I wasn't even there when they ate the apple! Yet, as I began to understand spiritual matters, I began to see that I was there just as a man and woman's children, grandchildren, great-grandchildren, and so on, are in the body of the man and woman in seed form before those descendants are actually born. In other words, in my children there is already the seed for their future children. In their future children will be the seed of their future children, and so on.

Now, as a parent, I can pass on to my children only what I am and what I possess. For example, if I speak only Chinese, I can pass on to my children only the Chinese language. I possess no other language to give them out of my own self. The same was true with Adam and Eve. Because they disobeyed God, their fellowship with God was broken. Therefore, their spirits died because they were severed from God. As a result, they could pass on to their children only a dead spirit—a sinful spirit, separated from God. And Adam and Eve's children could pass on to their children only a dead, sinful spirit. And so on, all the way down to you and me.

We said earlier that your spirit is the real you—who you really are. So what does it mean when your spirit—the real you—is separated from God? It means that unless you are somehow reconciled to God, you will go to hell after you die. Hell is a real place of real torment resulting from separation from God.

Now God is a holy God, and He will not tolerate sin in His Presence. At the same time, He is a loving God. Indeed, He IS Love! And because He loves you so much, He wanted to restore the broken relationship between you and Himself. He wanted to restore you to that glorious position of walking and talking with Him and enjoying the fullness of His blessings.

But there was a problem. Because God is infinite, only an infinite Being could satisfy the price of man's offense against God. At the same time, because man committed the offense, there had to be Someone Who would also be able to represent man in paying this price. In other words, there had to be a Being Who was both God and man in order that the price for sin could be paid.

Since God knew that there was nothing man could do on his own to pay the price for his sin, God took the initiative. In the writings of John the Apostle, we learn that "God so loved the world that He gave His only-begotten Son, that whoever believes in Him shall not perish but have eternal life" (John 3:16).

What glorious GOOD NEWS! God loved you so much that He sent His own and only Son, Jesus Christ, to take the rap for your sins. Imagine that! Would you give your son to go to the electric chair for someone else? Well, that's exactly what God did! The Cross was the electric chair of Christ's day, and God gave His own Son, Jesus Christ, to go to the Cross for you!

In dying on the Cross for you, and in rising from the dead three days later, Jesus paid the price for your sins and repaired the breach between you and God the Father. Jesus restored the broken relationship between man and God. He provided mankind with the gift of eternal life.

So what does all of this mean for you? It means that if you accept Christ's gift of eternal life, you will be "born again." In other words, God will replace your dead spirit with a spirit filled with His life. "Therefore, if anyone is in Christ, he is a new creation. The old has passed away; behold, the new has come" (2 Corinthians 5:17).

If I offer you a gift, it is not yours until you choose to take it. The same is true with the gift of eternal life. Until you choose to take it, it is not yours. In order for you to be born again, you must reach out and take the gift of eternal life that Jesus is offering you now. Here is how to receive it:

"Lord Jesus, I come to You now just as I am—broken, bruised, and empty inside. I've made a mess of my life, and I need You to fix it. Please forgive me of all of my sins. I accept You now as my personal Savior and as the Lord of my life. Thank You for dying for me so that I might live. As I give you my life, I trust that You will make of me all that You've created me to be. Amen."

If you prayed this prayer, please write to me to let me know. I will send you some information to help you get started in your Christian walk. Also, I encourage you to do three important things:

1) Get yourself a Bible and begin reading in the Gospel of John.

2) Find yourself a good church that preaches the full Gospel. Ask God to lead you to a church where you will be fed.

3) Set aside a time every day for prayer. Prayer is simply talking to God as you would to your best friend.

I congratulate you on making the life-changing decision to accept Jesus Christ! It is the most important decision of your life. Mark down this date because it is the date of your spiritual birthday. Be assured of my prayers for you as you grow in your Christian walk. God bless you!

Other Books by Dr. MaryAnn Diorio

A Christmas Homecoming

When Sonia Pettit's teenage daughter goes missing for seven long years, Sonia faces losing her mind, her family, and her faith.

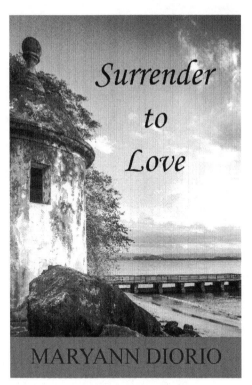

Surrender to Love

When young widow and life coach, Dr. Teresa Lopez Gonzalez, travels to Puerto Rico to coach the granddaughter of her mother's best friend, Teresa faces her unwillingness to surrender to God's will for her life. In the process, she learns that only by losing her life will she truly find it.

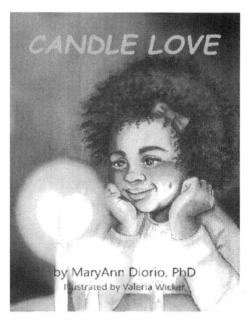

Candle Love

Four-year-old Keisha has a new baby sister. But Keisha doesn't want a new baby sister. Keisha is afraid that Mama will love Baby Tamara more than Mama loves her. But when Mama shows Keisha three special candles, Keisha learns that there is always enough love for everyone because the more one shares love, the more love grows.

Who Is Jesus?

Introduce your child to the true Jesus of the Bible.

Available in Kindle format.
Available in iPad format.
Available in Hardcover.
Available in Softcover.

Toby Too Small

Toby Michaels is small. Too small to be of much good to anyone. But one day, Toby discovers that it's not how big you are on the outside that matters; it's how big you are on the inside.

Available in hardcover, softcover, for Kindle and iPad.

Do Angels Ride Ponies?

A handicapped boy discovers the power of faith to achieve the impossible.

Available in Kindle Format.
Available in Softcover.

SOCIAL MEDIA SITES

You may find Dr. MaryAnn on the following Social Media Sites:

Website: www.maryanndiorio.com

Blog (Matters of the Heart): www.networkedblogs.com/blog/maryanndiorioblog

Amazon Author Central: www.amazon.com/author/maryanndiorio

Authors Den: www.authorsden.com/maryanndiorio

BookBub.com: www.bookbub.com/authors/maryann-diorio

Facebook: www.facebook.com/DrMaryAnnDiorio

Twitter: http://Twitter.com/DrMaryAnnDiorio

Goodreads: www.goodreads.com/author/show/6592603

LinkedIn: www.linkedin.com/profile/view?id=45380421

Pinterest: www.pinterest.com/drmaryanndiorio/

Google+: http://plus.google.com/u/0/+DrMaryAnnDiorio

Instagram: www.instagram.com/drmaryanndiorio/

Library Thing: www.librarything.com/profile/drmaryanndiorio

Vimeo: https://vimeo.com/user46487508

YouTube: www.youtube.com/user/drmaryanndiorio/

TopNotch Press
A Division of MaryAnn Diorio Books
PO Box 1185
Merchantville, NJ 08109
FAX: 856-488-0291
Email: info@maryanndiorio.com